C000017171

Miriam's Legacy

by

Patricia Rantisi

authorHOUSE®

AuthorHouse™ UK Ltd.
500 Avebury Boulevard
Central Milton Keynes, MK9 2BE
www.authorhouse.co.uk
Phone: 08001974150

© 2007 Patricia Rantisi. All rights reserved.

No part of this book may be reproduced, stored in a retrieval system, or
transmitted by any means without the written permission of the author.

First published by AuthorHouse 7/2/2007

ISBN: 978-1-4343-0412-4 (sc)
ISBN: 978-1-4343-0413-1 (hc)

Printed in the United States of America
Bloomington, Indiana

This book is printed on acid-free paper.

Cover design by Jane Greening.

In Memory of my husband Audeh,

who was himself a refugee

ONE

SHATILA REFUGEE CAMP, LEBANON 1982

Just about everyone was going about the camp whispering. "Granny, Um Tha'er, is *tabaneh*". It was whispered from person to person. Now, *tabaneh* in Arabic literally means 'tired' but sometimes it means 'dying'. It all depends on the inflection of the voice. This time people felt sure it meant that Granny was dying.

Few people knew exactly how old Granny was; she had never had any kind of birth certificate, nor was there any record of her birth but she always said she was born around the turn of the century, which would make her in her eighties, though she looked ninety. She could remember the rule of the Ottomans in Palestine and she had vivid memories of men wearing tall red tarbooshes with black tassels and long striped coat-gowns over baggy pantaloons. She could remember the Turkish soldiers riding so proudly on horseback and all the fanfare of their military parades. As far as I knew she was the oldest person in the refugee camp. She had survived the Turks, the British, the Israelis, and now the Lebanese.

Mostly she sat all day in the porch, her shrivelled up little body looking as if by the swish of a wand it would turn into stone. Her

1

sallow complexion and sunk in eyes only accentuated the hundreds of lines all over her face which made you want to bring out the iron to undo the crumpled creases. The wicker chair was cracking and split in various places and the legs looked as precarious as her own legs covered over by a knitted blanket. She was padded all around with innumerable coloured cushions, which had probably not been washed in aeons.

But her mind was still sharp and her memory alert. Granny was everyone's grandmother. Few girls of her generation had attended school, so she had never learnt to read or write; though in her younger days she knew how to calculate figures and was a dab hand at simple arithmetic. She was also very good at telling stories, some were folk tales, but most were true stories of life before the British took over Palestine. Some of the stories painted a picture of tranquillity, contentment and happiness in the rural life of Northern Palestine, though she had to admit they were not always peaceful times. There was always talk of a world war.

We wondered if, as Granny got older, she tended to embroider some of the stories to make them a little more colourful. Palestinians of Granny's generation imagined life as a paradise then, but in the eyes of present day, it would hardly be a paradise. More like paradise lost. The people were very poor, mostly village peasants, living very simple lives, close to the earth and living off the earth. Granny's family had kept two cows, a few goats and chickens, and a donkey, which was essential for travelling and transporting goods. They owned two small fields, in which they grew wheat and corn and a small patch for vegetables and herbs. This made them better off than most peasant families.

There was nothing I enjoyed more than sitting at Granny's feet and listening to her tales. Shatila refugee camp in the suburbs of Beirut, Lebanon, had been my world ever since I was born. I knew from my earliest days that I was Palestinian but not born in Palestine. I was born in Lebanon but not Lebanese.

As far as I could gather, Granny was my father's grandmother, which made her my great-grandmother. It was difficult for me to work out who was who with all the multiplication of generations.

It was just after my father had been taken away. The Lebanese were blaming us for the civil war in Lebanon, so they decided to get rid of all the Palestinian young men who had set up a base for the PLO in the refugee camps. Thousands were rounded up, their weapons still with them but their belongings scanty and some of them still wounded. They were literally thrown out, put on trucks, then herded on to ships at the port to say goodbye to Lebanon, but not to be repatriated to their beloved homeland of Palestine, only once more to be exiled to another part of the world. The authorities and international bodies had made assurances that those left behind, mainly women and children, would be protected. In fact, our beloved leader had declared, over and over, "Don't worry. I have asked for foreign armies to protect you all." Where the sons and fathers of families were going we did not know, but it was rumoured that their destination would be another Arab country, either Tunisia or Yemen.

I shall never forget my mother and older sister clinging on to my father's arm with fear and tears in their eyes. My stomach was churning over in knots. I wanted to scream but somehow I managed to hold myself together for my father's sake. After all he had told me to be brave and look after the family until he returned. Would he return? The other men did not seem very hopeful of a return. And besides at twelve, as I was then, how could I be responsible for my family? I tried to comfort my mother but she was utterly distraught. "What will become of us, Farres?" she cried. She was inconsolable.

My father, too, was trying to hide his emotions by words of encouragement that he would try to get back to us, as soon as possible and assuring us that we would be well looked after in the meantime. Little did we all envisage what was to come.

Just after this we heard that Granny was dying so we went to visit her. She had momentarily taken a turn for the better and was sitting up in bed; her beady eyes looking around at all the numerous relatives. She remembered me, even my name.   "Farres," she said, "you are the man of the house now, you have to grow up to be strong. Look after your mother and sisters, and never, never, never forget Palestine. I shall never go back, but one day, you will see our beloved homeland."

Then something extraordinary happened. At least, for me, it seemed extraordinary. Granny undid the pin on her bosom, holding together her gown, and handed the brooch to me. It was not an expensive piece of jewellery, just an enamel brooch in the design and colours of the Palestinian flag. To me it was of immense worth and to think out of all her children, grandchildren, and great-grandchildren I was chosen to carry the emblem of our nationality. I felt very privileged, but with a sense of responsibility. Then she put her hands under the blanket and fished out a very old string of glass worry beads in a blue-green mottled colour. "These were given to your great-grandfather by my very best friend's husband, a long, long time ago," she said, as she handed them to me.

I took the beads and kissed Granny's hand, thanking her. These two mementoes had no monetary value at all, but they were her legacy to me. On my way home I was trying to work out the significance of these seemingly worthless objects, and why I was her favourite. I had seen old men fingering strings of worry beads when they sat with nothing else to do. Sometimes they used them to pray. I did not notice until I reached home that the glass beads were different from most. When I examined them carefully, although they looked dirty and chipped, there was a small silver cross in between two of the beads. What did this mean, I wondered. I wished I had had the chance to ask Granny what it meant.

A few days later, Granny died peacefully. I don't remember too much about her funeral so I suppose it was a quiet affair. I only know that she was buried with great respect, all her relatives, and especially the 'elders' of the Camp attending. She had lived a long life but looking back, I was glad that she was spared the coming traumatic years of terror and humiliation.

* * * *

Mother did not believe me. "It can't be happening," was all she could say. She'd negated the rumours and even the noise of distant gunfire, yet I could see a pallor spreading over her face.

It had only been just over two weeks since the departure of my father. Mother was still trying to come to terms with all the grief and loss of him, wondering how she was going to cope. Now we were faced with a far worse tragedy.

One day a stranger suddenly intruded into our home kicking the door open and looking wilder than anyone I had ever seen. Her headscarf had obviously been snatched off her head and her long black hair was matted with blood and cement dust. She was cradling a baby in her arms but there was no sound coming from it. The woman's eyes were darting back and forth in a crazed manner and her speech was almost incoherent. I could see the poor woman was almost faint with shock, yet, at first, she refused to sit down. The smell from her dress told me why.

All she could utter was "The sports arena, the sports arena..." Then she started screaming with a shrill eerie cry, weeping, yet without tears. My mother, although far from calm herself, managed to pacify her and gave her a plastic chair with a cushion on it. I was shaking with fright and didn't know whether to stand or sit. My two younger sisters were still crouched together in a corner of the kitchen floor and my older sister had gone to visit a cousin in my aunt's house, which was the other side of the refugee camp. Up to now, we had not been worried about her.

"Fetch her a cup of water." My mother tried to relieve the poor deranged woman of the baby and I was glad to have something to do. The baby was reluctantly handed over. It was bundled up tightly with a blood-spattered blanket; its face barely visible. A low whimpering noise indicated that the baby was still alive as my mother sat down on the sitting room chair, covered with its velvet wall hanging of the Dome of the Rock in Jerusalem, to disguise the faded colours and broken springs of the once padded chair. It was the only upholstered chair in our family home. She placed the baby down in the crook of the chair and this made the child cry louder realising that it was no longer in the security of human arms. But it was not the cry of a normal baby with healthy lungs.

My mother stood up again, rocking the baby back and forth. Meanwhile, I couldn't take my eyes off this strange young woman whose hands and lips were trembling as she sipped the water. When she had placed the cup on the table she began to speak. Pointing to her black, outlined eyes, she said: "I have seen hell with these eyes, hell, hell, real hell, blood, fire, tanks, guns, bodies, your daughter…"

At this my mother started screaming. "Fatima, Fatima, what happened to her?"

"It's so terrible, I can't begin to tell you."

"What, what?" she shouted, shaking the woman and handing the baby to my sister. "How do you know it was Fatima?"

"They told me."

"Well, what happened, where can I find her?"

"She's dead. The soldiers took her clothes off, pinned her to the wall, raped her and then shot her."

This was too much. My mother collapsed in a heap on the floor. Soon all bedlam broke loose. We could hear screaming, shouting and scurrying feet outside the door. I opened it just a little to see a crowd of people, some carrying dead children with blood on their faces and clothes. It was horrible.

"Rape and massacre, murder and destruction." they shouted. At the time, I didn't know what rape meant, only that it was something violent and nasty. It was, indeed, mass murder on a grand scale. As more and more details emerged from various eye witnesses, the survivors were so stunned and disturbed that many had literally gone crazy.

Bodies were heaped on top of one another, girls stripped naked, children with limbs chopped off, pregnant women with their stomachs cut open, old men with their eyes gouged out, houses bulldozed on top of the bodies, some of them still with new paint on the doors. A sheer catalogue of evil.

Our visitor went on to recount how she had been crouching down sheltering from the gunfire under a low roof. She was right next to a young mother who was breast-feeding her baby. The mother was shot in the head and died instantly.

"I left her lying there and took the baby. This is not my baby," she said.

Early Sunday morning, just two days after the massacre, when we were assured that the gunmen and murderers had left, my mother pulled me out of bed hushing me not to wake up my sisters. Quickly dressing, we left the house quietly and walked through the narrow alleyways, garnished with trash of every description. We were soon greeted by a crowd of wailing women, covering their eyes and mouths with their headscarves.

The stench of death made my stomach heave. Some of the women were literally vomiting, but my mother just clung to me searching vainly with her eyes for some glimpse amongst all the corpses for her dead daughter. I, too, was scanning the piles of bodies. There was a young girl who I could barely recognise because the body was bloated and bluish-grey, but did I see a small birthmark close to her right ear? I couldn't be sure but I decided not to point her out to my mother. I did not say anything.

Soon, the cries and wails were deafened by the noise of bulldozers and we found ourselves standing on the edge of a big crater that had been dug as a grave. Men with white uniforms with bold red crosses and white masks covering their faces were ordering everyone to leave the area. We stood at a distance watching the bulldozers scoop up the bodies; men, women, children and babies, and dump them into their common ignoble grave. Apart from the horror, these were people. Mothers and fathers, brothers and sisters. Didn't they deserve a proper funeral like Granny, at least?

Later we talked to a woman who had lost her parents, her daughter, a bride with her newly wed husband, her own husband, uncles, cousins and many others of her extended family who had perished. She was so disorientated she couldn't comprehend how she alone had survived. Some people had been hidden from view but had been eye witnesses to the terrible atrocities. It was a merciful end if you were just lined up against the wall and shot dead. The unspeakable horrors were of men and women chopped up with axes and mothers forced to watch the murder of their terrified children.

At least we were only mourning the loss of my sister, I thought. The house was filled for weeks afterwards with well-meaning, sympathetic relatives who came to condole us but who also had tragic stories to tell. Meanwhile my mother could not eat, sleep, talk or even think for many days. All she could console herself with was that Fatima was a martyr and that I, as her only son, was still alive.

* * * *

I suppose at that time, like all young boys, I had a vivid imagination. In spite of all the terrible horrors and tragedies we had experienced, I tried to be strong and optimistic. What I had personally witnessed would turn the stomach green and the mind black of any normal human being.

I remember, one day, I was wearing my brand new sneakers, given by some foreign charity. The soles of my others were completely threadbare, and already the new ones had been scuffed as I kicked at the stones and jumped into the little rain puddles. I made up a game of counting the puddles and examining them for beetles, spiders and other tiny creatures. I had always been fascinated by anything alive from tiny insects to animals and birds, to humans and the way they ticked. I wanted to discover more and more about nature, the diversity of it, how creatures reproduced, how babies were born; life and death. There was so much to learn.

I was enjoying my little walk, only a few yards away from home. There were narrow alleyways barely wide enough for one person to squeeze through but certainly not wide enough for two people to pass each other. My mother had sent me on an errand to the corner shop to buy kerosene for her Primus, some matches, and cubes of chicken stock, which she said had probably never seen a chicken but at least gave a little flavour to her cooking. There were two coins left, so I bought some chewing gum, a real luxury.

My errand should have taken me only ten minutes at the most, but having been cooped up in my cramped home for weeks and with the first shower of rain I couldn't get enough of the cool fresh air. So

I dawdled. I imagined myself in wide-open spaces, playing football with my friends. "I wish, I wish," I said aloud. Then my eye caught sight of a miniature army of ants, following each other in a long line and carrying pieces of something larger than themselves. I decided to examine them closer and follow them to their source. At first it looked like dead leaves, then I realised that it was tiny bits of old rags. The ants had emerged from a pile of dirt and concrete.

This used to be someone's home; I thought, now demolished and desolate. As I got closer, I was almost knocked back by the smell, but I started rummaging under a heap of stones nearby and found, to my horror, remains of a baby's hand, bloodied and blue but wrapped in a piece of cotton, which had once been white. Just then my mother's voice suddenly brought my reveries to a halt.

"Farres, Farres, O God where are you?" she called.

I wasn't sure what to do, but decided to carry my find home and give it a proper burial. After all, it once belonged to a human baby and deserved a decent burial.

"Where on earth have you been all this long time?"

My mother's face showed a range of emotions, first anger, then relief and finally disgust, when I showed her my find. "Allah, preserve us," she exclaimed. My two younger sisters rushed to the door. They would be happy to see their brother scolded, I thought. Any little bit of excitement was a welcome space from boredom.

"Yes, what on earth have you been up to?"

"What is that nasty pong?" Farida said, puckering up her nose.

"I've been watching a colony of ants."

"Ants?"

"Yes, ants. They are so organised, like an army and carrying bits of stuff much bigger and heavier than themselves."

Farida started to laugh, mockingly. "Ants are just dirty *dud*. You should have stepped on them and killed them all."

"Have pity, they are small and defenceless".

"But they are stupid creatures, they have no brains."

"How do you know?"

"Well, I would have stepped on them!"

"I nearly did too. Then I thought that's what we were like when the Israelis and Phalangists came. We were defenceless. They massacred us. If I'd stepped on the ants, that would have been another massacre."

"Silly philosopher, silly, silly, silly", chanted Fayrouz my other sister as she clapped her hands.

"Well, shouldn't we consider preparing and arming ourselves for defence in case our enemy strikes again?" I said.

"Now, you're talking sense," chorused my two sisters.

My mother, however, shuddered at the thought of guns in the house. Her thin frail body began to shiver at such a suggestion. Anyway, I gave Mama the plastic can of kerosene and the other purchases and went into the house. The delicious aroma of freshly baked bread filled my nostrils with delight overcoming the other horrible smells. But I decided to dig a hole in the earthen lane to give the baby's hand a decent burial first. How ironic, I thought that I could bury a stranger baby's hand and not be allowed to bury my own sister.

My mother had worked herself up with worry and anger and had decided to scold and even punish me for being so slow and longwinded, but all she could say was "Thank God you're back safe,"

It had never occurred to me before that we Palestinians always have the name of God on our lips, never as a curse or sacrilegious blasphemy but a belief that God had ordained our destiny and we only had to fear Him, whatever happened. Our home was a small two roomed flat in

11

a concrete block where many other families lived and we had to thank God that we still had a home.

After finishing my task I washed my hands and started to nibble on the thin, flat loaves my mother had baked.

"Wait, I'm making soup, if you eat all the bread now, there won't be any left to eat with the soup," she declared.

So, holding my hungry stomach, I waited. It was *fareeki* soup, made of green wheat grains and flavoured with the chicken cubes.

We had not seen chicken or any other kind of meat for months.

After lunch, I went to the cupboard and fished out my shoebox with my little treasures. I examined again the small brooch and the string of beads that Granny had given me, trying to see if there was any significance in them. The glass beads were so old and dirty that some of them were chipped and had lost their sheen, but I fingered them round my hand reciting some prayers from the Koran. I was glad that Granny had died just before the massacre. I wondered what her life had been like before she came to Lebanon. Who was that special best friend, I wondered. I remembered asking my father some time ago what Granny's real name was because she had always been known by the name of her first-born son Tha'er, as is the custom.

Her real name was Miriam…

Two

NORTHERN PALESTINE 1912

A new dawn was breaking in a northern village of Palestine, situated on a rocky hill with a view of the Mediterranean Sea on a clear day. The sound of squawking seabirds aroused young Miriam from sleep and she stepped outside. She was mesmerized by the sight of the morning mist slowly rising from the ground like a shroud that had covered the dark, dry earth all night, leaving it glistening in a shaft of light coming from a sun that was just waking up.

The silvery olive trees, already beginning to look laden with the green olives seemed to beckon her, as was the orchard of fruit trees heavily pregnant with apples. But it was too early for the olive harvest and today was not a day for picking fruit. It was a day for growing up.

Miriam did not want to grow up. She was a wild, free spirit, and if she had had her own way, she would have run in the orchard with her black hair flowing and her long skirts flapping in the breeze. She knew that she could only do that in her dreams. In her dreams, she was always running, skipping and sometimes even flying a few feet off the ground through fields and forests, riding on the crests of waves near the shore, exploring the wide, wide, world of which she knew so little.

Her world was very small. It consisted of her home, her family, village life, and a once-in-a-blue-moon visit to the coastal city of Haifa. Her family home was built of quarried stone with each stone chiselled by hand, topped by a flat cement roof. There was one large living room, used also for sleeping, a kitchen room on one side and a storeroom on the other, opening onto a large courtyard with a well in the middle. An overgrown fig tree and a lemon tree adorned the courtyard.

Miriam's daily routine centred around helping her mother look after the other children, and preparing the food for storage in the winter. The rhythmic regularity of everyday life, in season and out of season was sometimes interspersed with religious feasts or family occasions such as weddings and funerals. Today was going to be different. At age twelve, it was the occasion of her betrothal.

She tiptoed quietly around her mother who was prostrate on her prayer mat performing her morning religious ritual in the middle of the room. No doubt she was praying for Miriam to be happy with the young man who had been chosen for her to spend the rest of her life with.

His name was Amin and he lived in the next village. In fact they were second cousins; their grandfathers were brothers. Amin was fifteen, just three years older than herself, a nice looking young lad with dark hair combed straight back from his forehead to disguise the wiry curls which sprang back at his temples when he laughed. And he laughed a lot, which was one thing that Miriam liked about him. His dark skin had soft fuzz but it hadn't reached the stage yet for making it necessary for him to shave. Both of them were still innocent children. Miriam had not started her periods or developed breasts, but she was growing tall and strong. Above all, she was wholesome and had healthy looking skin, which her future in-laws had noted very carefully. Most importantly, like her mother, she was likely to embrace motherhood easily and breed without complications.

Amin's family had come to congratulate Miriam's parents at her birth, bringing trays of sweet pastries and gold bracelets signifying that they looked forward to the day when their son, then only three, would become engaged to this beautiful new baby girl. Now that day had arrived.

Miriam was excited, nervous, yet sad at the same time. Growing up and marriage was only for grown-ups. She wanted to enjoy her freedom as a child, longer.

"I have been dreading this day for weeks, but now I am going to enjoy it. I am going to be a princess for one day!" Miriam announced to no one in particular, although her little sister was looking at her with a mischievous grin on her face.

"Don't you spoil it for me with your naughty ways." Both of them giggled as if they had discovered a secret.

"Stop messing around, you have to have a bath and I am going to make sure it is all done properly." Miriam's mother was always bossing everyone around and this day more than any other she wanted everyone to know that she was in charge. A zinc bath was filled with warm water, heated in the kitchen, and Miriam was sponged all over with olive oil soap, including her hair.

"Ow, gently, Mama, you are scrubbing me too hard and I've got soap in my eyes". "Oh, grow up," said her mother sternly. Miriam could not help noticing that although outwardly her mother appeared distant, she had tears in her eyes.

"Are you crying, Mama?"

"No, Just noticing that you will soon be a lady. And soon you will belong to another family."

"But I will always be your daughter".

"Yes, darling," said her mother, planting a wet kiss on her forehead.

Then she started shouting orders to the rest of the family and other relatives. Miriam's father had helped prepare the two sheep the day before, stuffing them with rice, meat, nuts and spices. They were ready for roasting.

"Have you carried the sheep to the baker's oven yet?"

"Have you prepared the lemonade?"

"Have you fried the pine-nuts and almonds? Be careful not to burn them."

"Have you finished ironing Miriam's dress?"

"Have the chickens been fed?"

"Has the yoghurt set?"

Everyone was rushing around to get the house and courtyard tidy before Amin and his relatives arrived. Later that afternoon, Miriam was seated in the best chair, looking regal in her new colourful embroidered dress and discreet makeup, her head covered with a huge fringed shawl that hung well down over her shoulders and revealing underneath it a headband of a cluster of silver coins. The chair beside her was empty.

Someone struck up a chord on the '*oud*' or five-stringed Palestinian fiddle and another young girl beat out the rhythm with her hands on a drum made of animal skin that was stretched over a clay pot. The older women started the dancing, waving coloured scarves and handkerchiefs in the air and whirling around using their feet, hips and arms, bobbing their heads and clapping their hands. Some of the women were ululating from their throats, making the piercing joy cry. Almost all of the village were there, Christian neighbours as well as immediate family and Muslim friends. Miriam's special friend, Majida was there too. Majida was older but her marriage had not yet been arranged. They had spent their childhood together and Majida wondered if they would be parted now.

"*Mubruk, Mubruk,* Congratulations!" Majida hugged Miriam and noted that her friend had tears with all the emotion of the day. She wasn't sure whether to laugh or cry, herself.

Finally, the men arrived, Amin looking very smart in his Western-style dark suit and white shirt. He was seated next to Miriam. Bouquets of flowers were arranged around so that the couple looked like they were sitting in a garden. Then relatives presented Miriam with gold bracelets, necklaces and earrings, wishing her a happy future. The house was so full, no one could move and it seemed the roof would burst with all the singing, clapping, and cries of joy.

The evening finished with a big feast of roast lamb in the courtyard, everyone sitting on stools or on the floor. There were all sorts of spicy salads, yogurt, and bread, all laid out on huge metal trays with the meat and stuffing. The older men were served first, rolling the rice into little balls with their hands and tossing them into their mouths. It was Miriam's brothers and other young men who were doing the serving, for once the women taking it easy until it came to the time for clearing up. What a feast, what joy, what chaos and what a mess after it was all over!

* * * *

Following the engagement, the elders of the two families decided to postpone the wedding for at least another year, which was a relief to both Miriam and Amin. Actually Miriam's fears of being restricted turned out to be unfounded. Girls were strictly protected by their families but in some ways Miriam found she was freer than before. Although still living with her parents and under their authority, they never refused her permission to visit Amin in the next village, which was less than one hour's walk away. One of her brothers, of whom she had three older than herself, accompanied her on the walk. Sometimes, Amin visited her and they sat together in the courtyard and talked about how life was going to be for them both.

"Will I be able to come home sometimes?"

"Of course," Amin laughed nervously. "And your parents will visit you, when you are settled in my home. My mother is looking forward to having you around."

"Will she expect me to help look after your brothers and sisters?"

"No, but she will expect you to help in the kitchen. Can you cook?"

"Of course I can. But your mother might do things differently than my mother,"

"Well, you may have to learn new ways,"

* * * *

Spring had come early but the last storm of winter the night before had played havoc in the garden and orchard. The strong winds and torrential rain had lashed against the young trees so that many of the sapling branches had broken and lay wounded, and the pink and white petals of the almond blossoms covered the ground like snow. Only the gnarled old olive trees, some of them hundreds of years in age seemed unharmed by the storm. Suddenly the sun came out and warmed up the damp earth, exuding a pungent smell, but the mud paths would take days to dry out.

Miriam was sitting on a stool outside the kitchen picking through trays of lentils and rice on her lap, at the same time keeping an eye on her younger brother and sister who were running around chasing each other, when she heard an alarming scream. It was Majida who rushed into their courtyard, her eyes red and wide and her hair dishevelled. "Please fetch your mother," she shouted to Miriam.

"Whatever is the matter?"

"Oh, it's terrible, my baby brother has fallen down the well. He's dead,"

Two of Miriam's brothers and her parents rushed over to the neighbours to find them already wailing and tearing at their hair and garments. There was nothing they could do except sit and try to comfort the family. Apparently, the little toddler had dropped a toy into the well and climbed over the parapet to try to retrieve it, losing his balance. It was all very sad. Already the priest had been sent for to arrange the burial.

The memories of that day remained forever with Miriam. The angelic body of that little boy lying in the wooden box, his pale face surrounded by wild anemones and cyclamen, an icon of Jesus and a rosary draped across his tiny chest; the wailing cries of his mother and Majida, the quiet weeping of his father and brother; the priest in lengthy black robes, his long white hair tied back in a bun, covered with a tall black hat, reciting prayers from a book, the gold cross hanging down from his neck; the candles; the community of Christians singing chants as they carried the small coffin to the church and then the silent march back to the house after the burial; the whispering; the clink of coffee cups; then the smell of coffee.

"Do you realise that my little brother's name was Issa, which means Jesus, and your name is Miriam the Mother of Jesus? So we are related in a way, even though you are Muslim and I am Christian." Majida suddenly said.

Miriam had never thought about their differences in religion before. Her friend's announcement quietly shocked her and she didn't know quite how to respond to this but she gave her friend a big hug.

"Yes, you'll always be more than my friend," she said, "we are sisters!"

Muslims, Christians and Jews were always helping one another out in times of family crises. There was no religious animosity or distinction between them. Were they not all Palestinians under the rule of the Turkish Ottomans? Whether the occasion was a time of bereavement and called for condolences, or whether it was a time of celebration for a wedding, everyone made it their duty to join in. Religious feasts were times of celebration and social intercourse. Whenever there was a special need, any available financial help was shared if possible, and hospitality was never questioned or denied. It never occurred to Miriam's family, or any other for that matter to save money for a 'bad day'. The only thing people saved for was wedding celebrations.

* * * *

Her parents had not told Miriam the facts of life, though she had gleaned some information from her friend, and watched the farm animals have their babies. She knew that baby chickens came from eggs, but she did not know that unfertilised eggs didn't produce chicks.

"Mama, how are babies made?" she asked her mother one day in the kitchen. Her mother turned, acutely embarrassed.

"God makes babies and anything else you need to know your husband will tell you when the time comes," was all she would say. Miriam sighed and determined to ask Amin the next time she saw him.

"Amin, tell me, how are we going to make babies?" she suddenly came out with as they took a walk around the herb garden. He was so shocked. Could it be that his wife to be was so innocent? He didn't know quite how to answer her.

"Hasn't your mother told you all those things?"

"No," she said. "Mama said you would tell me,"

"Well," he said, "on our wedding night we will come together. For you it will hurt the first time and there will be a little blood. My father will be waiting to see the blood on the sheet."

It all sounded frightful, but she dared not ask any more questions. Amin decided to change the subject.

"Shall I tell you a story," he said, trying to lighten the situation.

"Oh, yes please," Miriam replied.

Amin had been to school and could read and write but these were Arabic folk tales that had never been written down. They had been passed down through the generations.

They sat under an old olive tree next to the herb garden with its exterior roots making a kind of seat. Amin felt his emotions charged and aroused, so he did not want to sit too close to Miriam, but she grabbed his arm and wanted to hold his hand. Anyway, there were too many family eyes watching. He began nervously:

> Once upon a time there was a royal family. Their children had all died except for one daughter called Dunya. This princess grew up to be a dazzling beauty hearing nothing but words of praise and admiration from all. As a consequence she grew very proud and haughty. She rejected all the suitors who wanted to marry her.
>
> Finally the son of her uncle who was King in another country came to ask for her hand. Since they were cousins and because their marriage would unite the two kingdoms, both families were overjoyed at the prospect.
>
> Dunya agreed to the marriage and the legal documents were drawn up and signed, the planned wedding to take place in ten days time. But Dunya hadn't yet met the prince and one of her maids spied him through a crack in the door of his room.
>
> "Come, Princess Dunya, and watch your new husband through a crack in the door", said the maid. Dunya peeped through the crack and saw the well-dressed young man eating a pomegranate. She saw a seed fall on the rug and watched as the young man picked it up and put it in his mouth.

She was trembling with rage and ran to her father. "Is this the man you wish me to marry?" she burst out. "Why he's no more than Bug, son of a Bug, who picks seeds from the rug. He behaves like a beggar or a beast."

"Calm yourself, daughter," the King said. "This is a sign that he is humble enough not to waste God's good fruit."

However, Dunya wouldn't listen to reason and utterly refused to continue with the wedding plans. Prince Safwan was understandably angry.

"Very well, Uncle", he said. "She says I'm Bug, son of a Bug who picks up seeds from the rug, while she is so lofty and proud. Let her remain unmarried and I shall find another wife." The next day he returned home with his soldiers and servants.

"What a horrible princess." interrupted Miriam.

"Yes, but wait, she will be punished."

Amin continued:

Dunya's father spoke sternly to his daughter and banished her to a small palace with a large garden and lots of servants. He told her she could stay in her own palace with whatever she needed but without the love and care of her parents.

Prince Safwan travelled all day long but did not reach his home. He decided to avenge himself on this haughty, presumptuous girl by tricking her. He ordered his soldiers to pitch their tents and live as civilian travellers, buying food from the nearby village and staying in that place until he returned. He then dressed in simple clothes and returned to the city on foot, refusing even to take his horse.

On his way, he met a gypsy carrying a musical instrument.

"Look," he suggested to the gypsy, "suppose you were to sell me your *rabab* and change clothes with me? I'll give you five dinars as well." The gypsy was pleased. Next, the prince had to learn how to play the instrument and also darken his skin with a dye to make him look like a gypsy. He called himself Hajji Brumbock. He composed love songs and performed every day for many people, including the servants from Dunya's palace.

Dunya heard about this wonderful new gypsy singer and told her personal maid Massada to bring him to a corner of her garden to sing to her personally. When he reached the palace garden he danced around, greeting the princess respectfully. She addressed him with contempt at first but then she became utterly entranced with his music and words of praise for her beauty. She decided that he should remain at the palace and sing for her alone. "But, your Highness", he protested, "I need to earn my living." She told him she would double his normal salary and give him food and lodging. He accepted and began to live in the servant's quarters.

"This is getting exciting", Miriam exclaimed, her face glowing. Amin continued:

Gradually, she felt attracted to him so much that she invited him into her private room at the palace. She gave him a new suit and talked to him as if he were a friend. But Hajji Brumbrock complained to her that he was still sleeping in the servant's quarters. Little by little she raised his status so that she forgot her royal rank. She had fallen madly in love with him and as his songs and poems became more passionate she gave in to his polite entreaties to share her bed.

"Wow, so they were…like… kind of married." Miriam was beginning to understand.

"Yes. Let me continue…"

'One day, after two and a half months, he donned his old clothes and told her he was leaving to go back to his old country. She started to cry and plead with him.

"Don't leave me alone, Hajji Brumbrock. I'm going to have a child and my father will kill me if he finds out".

"He'll kill me too, that's why I must flee", he replied.

"No, take me with you", she pleaded.

"You are a princess. You fell in love with a gypsy but you were legally married to your cousin Prince Safwan. You cannot leave the palace and live the life of a gypsy".

She continued to plead, weeping and grabbing his tattered clothes. Finally, he consented, on condition that she leave her jewels and fine clothes and dress as a gypsy woman. They left by cover of darkness and he changed his tone of voice and attitude towards her. He spoke to her roughly and she had to endure hunger, thirst and weariness, walking on foot. When he brought her food it was mixed up unappetizingly and she had to eat with her fingers.

"And do you know what else he did?" Amin was laughing. He obviously thought it very funny but Miriam was taking it so seriously.

"No, what?"

'Dunya asked for pudding, so he brought her some and then he threw it onto a rock and forced her to lick it off the rock".

"Ugh, how filthy"!

24

Amin continued again:

After a while he took pity on her and gave her a donkey to ride but still treated her in a churlish manner. She was deeply hurt and utterly exhausted, but did not dare complain. He left her in a cave while he went to search for the soldiers he had left behind, telling them to go on ahead and he would follow.

They journeyed on until they came to the King's palace. He continued to humiliate and torment her leaving her in the stable of the palace until the child was born.

"How much more cruel can he get, she didn't deserve all that!" said Miriam.

"Yes, I agree, He was rather cruel, now listen to what happens next…"

Then his mother, the Queen, who had been told the truth, brought her to the palace with the new baby. Prince Safwan came in and saw her in the royal bed.

"Who is this? It's the wife of Hajji Brumbrock. In my bed!" Then he went laughing up to Dunya, now so confused, "Yes", he said, "I'm Bug, son of a Bug, who picked seeds from the rug. And you're Lady Brumbrock who licked the pudding off the rock."

Then she realised who he really was and that he was her legal husband. She confessed that she had treated him badly and he also asked her forgiveness for his cruelty to her. They lived happily ever after.

At the end of the story, Miriam sat with her head bowed and seemed upset.

"Are you crying, silly? It's only a fairy story. In real life things don't happen that way."

She looked up with damp eyes and found him laughing quietly, his black curls bouncing on his forehead. He looked at her and smiling put his arm around her shoulder. "I will be a good husband." he said. "I love you, Miriam."

She was ecstatic and wanted to hug him, but he took her by the hand and led her into the courtyard. "Time for supper, go and help your mother," he said.

* * * *

Miriam had been engaged for about six months when it happened. She was picking some vegetables in the garden one morning when she suddenly felt something trickle down her legs. She rushed to the latrine and to her horror found it was blood. She had not been warned about periods, and she remembered what Amin had told her. How come I have blood before my wedding night, what am I to do? She thought.

She rushed over to Majida's and found her in the garden. Majida laughed when Miriam told her her fears and explained everything. "This is the feminine pest, all women have this once a month. It can be bothersome and sometimes unpleasant," she said. "Now, go home to your mother and ask her to give you some clean rags. I'm sure it will signify a celebration of sorts because it means you are now a woman." Miriam felt ashamed and dirty but was astonished at the reaction of her mother when she whispered to her what was happening. Her mother started to yodel the joy cry making the rest of the family rush to see what was the cause for a signal of celebration.

"Thank God," they all cried. "Miriam is now grown up!"

THREE

━━━━━━━━━━━━━━━━━━━━━━━

SHATILA CAMP 1985

Three years on from the massacre and my mother was still grieving, not just because Fatima had died but because she did not see her body or was able to bury her. She never stopped blaming herself for letting Fatima out of the house alone. We could not understand at first why she had gone to that fatal area of the Camp. Later we were told that there had been a march of young women and girls to protest the presence of Israeli troops who had been going round the perimeters of the Camp for several days. Probably she had been persuaded by others to join in the demonstration, never guessing for one second that they would all be murdered by Lebanese Phalangist militia and egged on by Israeli soldiers. In fact several bits of information emerged after their evil deeds had been analysed. It appeared that Lebanese militia were totally drunk and depraved as they used their machine guns and axes to murder innocent women and children. People had told us of finding empty whisky bottles thrown amongst the bodies.

Fatima was not yet fifteen years old at the time, about the same age as I was in 1985. By this time I knew what rape meant and turned over in my mind what Fatima must have gone through. The boys at school used to snigger and tell stories of sex, dirty tales, a subject supposed to be taboo in our society. They told me it was better that Fatima died for no man would marry her after that experience.

Now we were faced with new horrors. The Amal militias were murdering our people. There was shelling, bombing and shooting daily. I began to think, 'Where is God?' 'What is our crime as Palestinians?' I could no longer pray any more. First the Israelis, who are Jews, then the Phalangists, who are Christians, and now the Amal, Muslims like ourselves, who once stood with us, were now killing us. I wanted to scream, shout and curse. "Allah, Allah, damn you, damn."

My mother turned round from her kitchen chores, horrified.

"Shush, shame on you talking like that, you mustn't blame God", she said.

"I don't believe in God anymore, what's He ever done to help us? Jews, Christians and Muslims all profess to pray and respect God and look what's happening. I hate them all. Even our own brothers are against us now. Are we vermin?"

My mother was taking this personally and facing me her eyes pleading said, "Please don't talk like that son, you're all I have. Don't get so angry. Don't even think about getting yourself a gun."

I hugged her, sensing a deep tenderness and compassion, her fragile form felt so vulnerable. I was taller than she was and still growing but I could feel her shoulder blades and bony ribcage. Still so young and I could see her hair peeping out from her headscarf was already turning grey. I had heard her cough in the sleepless nights. What would become of us if she died? I couldn't bear to think about it.

"Mama, you are not taking care of yourself and don't worry they won't let me carry a gun. They say I am too young."

The Camp Wars, as they were called, had been going on for months. Nowhere was safe. I felt responsible for my mother and two sisters so I tried to think of a safer place for them to hide. But my mother was stubborn and adamant. She wanted to stay in the house, whatever happened. The Palestinian fighters and Amal militia were fighting it out in the streets, shooting each other in the alleyways, using bits of corrugated metal for shields and crouching behind banks of dirty sand and rubble. Every building had sandbags around it. Every day the casualties mounted up.

Arms had been smuggled into the Camp over a long period and some of the men who had been evacuated managed to return to fight, though mostly it was the youths who were fighting. I wanted desperately to join in. Yet I knew it was too dangerous and I had to admit that when I saw what was going on I did not feel very brave. I was scared. I would sometimes lie flat on my stomach on the flat roof of our building, and watch.

One day, as the sun was going down and the full moon was already high in the sky there seemed to be an atmosphere of doom. It was quiet at first, even the dogs had stopped barking, but then a lot of dogs had already died. Some dogs had been shot, others died of hunger and others, a ghastly thought, had landed up on dinner tables. Suddenly, there was a big boom. A house at the end of the street had been hit by a rocket and the people started tumbling out of the front entrance screaming and panicking. A small boy was looking very dazed and was bleeding from his shoulder, his mother too weak to help him. She was struggling to stand up, hanging on to the electricity wires, which hung in huge groups of ropes, outside the buildings. With their insulated plastic coverings they had always reminded me of spaghetti.

Without a second thought, I ran down the stairs and along the road to see if I could help. Mama followed me yelling, "Farres, Farres."

"Get me some clean rags," I yelled back.

She ran home and returned with an old sheet and somehow, I knew instinctively what to do. I tore up the sheet and wrapped it round the boys arm and shoulder, as tight as I could. The bleeding stopped, and after a while the medics arrived and carried him to the makeshift clinic.

"Well done, good lad," they said to me.

"For once, you have been useful," Mama said, putting her arm around me. "You have been so bad, so sulky and so rebellious lately."

"Damn, hell, what else do you expect me to be."

"And stop using that language."

"Yes, Mother."

Every night, as a family of four we clung together on the thin mattresses on the concrete floor, covering ourselves with blankets. We listened to the sounds of tanks rumbling by, the whizz of bullets and the boom of explosives. Sometimes, my uncle, my mother's brother, and his family would come down from their home upstairs to join us, so that we were often ten or twelve people huddled together, trying to keep warm by the closeness of our bodies, but with our stomachs rumbling with hunger. Food seemed to be the dominant subject of conversation, indeed it seemed to occupy our thoughts day and night. Questions were in the order of:

"Can anyone tell me how I can make two eggs enough for all of us?"

"Yes, got any flour? Mix it with water and flour and make pancakes."

"But there is not enough oil for frying!"

"Anyway, where did you find the eggs? All the chickens have been killed."

"Does anyone have an onion? There is some grass and dandelions on that waste ground over there."

"And how do you think you can risk going out to pick them?"

"I hear some people are eating the flesh of cats and dogs and even rats."

"Ugh, ugh! There were audible sounds of disgust from everyone.

I had remembered that my mother had made a stew once, which had bits of meat floating in it and she had actually found an onion to flavour it. I questioned her many times as to where the meat came from but she would not tell me. I did not like to think about it, only that we found it delicious. Perhaps because we were so hungry.

I guess I couldn't altogether hide the fact that I disliked my uncle intensely. I could never see any connection or likeness between him and my mother, yet I knew they were brother and sister. Perhaps it was his large nose that seemed to take up his whole face especially as his frontal hair was receding. Perhaps it was jealousy, that around the same age as my father, he had not been taken away like the other men of his generation. He had not been a fighter for the PLO as my father had been and at the time of the deportation he had feigned illness. True, he was not strong physically, but then he smoked constantly as nearly all the men did. Now, under siege, it was more important for him to have his cigarettes than the children to have bread. What's more he was always shouting at his wife and family. My father had been much more caring. How I missed him now.

Our candles had run out, so we could do nothing in the evenings except sit and tell each other stories or jokes.

One night my Aunt began:

"Once upon a time there lived an old woman in a hut in a forest. Everyone in the village was afraid of her and said she was a witch who used to cast spells on people. She used to lure the children of the village by giving them sweets. Indeed her house was built of sweets, sticky toffees, chocolate bars, liquorice sticks, bubbly pink powders, yellow popcorn, sugar-coated almonds and all stuck together with chewing gum."

My sisters and young cousins were sitting eagerly listening, and although dark, I could almost sense their mouths watering. This is cruel, I thought. We had not seen any kind of sweets for weeks and now my uncle's wife was unfairly making our mouths water. Anyway, it was a fun distraction.

"Once lured into the candy house, the children would be locked up as prisoners and had to work as slaves for the old woman," my aunt continued.

"But their parents became worried and gathered together in the village square to plan how they could get their children back. They decided to cut down the trees surrounding the house, so the sun would melt the sweets and chocolate. So a group of them went into the forest with axes to chop down the trees..."

Just then a deafening explosion rocked our house and we were all knocked sideways. A small crack appeared above our heads and we found ourselves covered in a sticky mess of concrete dust, water and oil.

"See, the house is melting," someone shouted. We couldn't help but laugh.

"I wish it was chocolate," another child shouted.

We were still laughing when things had calmed down and we edged our way up the stairs to find a missile had struck and made a large gap in the kitchen wall. It had punctured the water pipe and shattered a large glass jar half-full of olive oil. That was the end of our laughter, when we saw all the mess and we remembered that grandma had been left in bed. We rushed into her room and found her badly shaken but unharmed.

My mother set to, to help them clear up but we only had the light of a small torch. We decided the family must all come downstairs to sleep in our flat, as it was not only dangerous but far too cold in their home. They were reluctant to take advantage of our offer at first.

"We will manage, besides grandma will not budge. She says she will die in her own bed," my uncle said.

"No, I insist, go and fetch your mattresses and blankets. Let us try and get some sleep tonight at least. We don't know what tomorrow will bring," my mother said.

Finally they were persuaded and so our family grew overnight and stayed like that for some time to come.

We had been under siege for six months and the situation was getting steadily worse. Children were dying from hunger or lack of medical care. The hospital had been bombed and some of the health workers killed. Volunteer doctors were arriving from Europe to help so the world was beginning to take notice. Some poor women had sneaked out of the Camp at night to try and find food and then had been shot when they tried to return with bags of rice or sugar. It was a miserable existence.

Some of my classmates had joined the fighters even though they were not much older than me. I soon heard that one of my friends had been badly injured.

I had been watching carefully a group of Amal soldiers in a half-bombed out building. They sat near the checkpoint at the entrance to the Camp, relaxed, yet no doubt planning their next move. They had thought it would be easy to over run the Camp within a short time. Now months had passed and they still faced fierce resistance and stubborn steadfastness from the Palestinians. They had not expected us to resist and were surprised to see our firearms. I used to watch them from the roof of a neighbour's building, but made sure they did not see me watching them. If only I had a little hand-grenade I could throw it in their midst, frighten them and then steal their Kalashnikovs.

I decided to find out where the youths were hiding weapons, but knew I had to be careful because I did not want them to get into trouble. I sneaked out one evening, when all was quiet and following my instincts found a dugout basement. It was partially hidden by sandbags and as I removed the bit of corrugated iron used as a makeshift entrance I started to tremble. What if the militias have followed me? Not only would I be in trouble but the other kids would get shot. I covered my head with my worn raincoat and slid down the mud opening. The boys were not much older than myself. They stared at me open-mouthed, as their small lamp flickered in the dark.

"Hell, what do you want, you idiot?"

"I need a hand grenade…just a small one," I stammered.

"Are you mad? We don't have grenades. Get out of here!"

"Yes, get out quick, before we kick you."

"And not a word to anyone." The last word was from a kid I recognised from school.

His name was Mohammed and he followed me out. He spoke more kindly than the others did but warned me not to tell a soul where they were hiding.

Disappointed, I returned home and made up some excuse to my mother for my disappearance. As usual, she was worried sick. I kept thinking and plotting what I could do. The idea came to me in the middle of the night. I would hurl a big rock into their midst and then when the soldiers scattered, I would snatch a gun. It all seemed so easy.

* * * *

I was sitting on the bank of the river...or was it the ocean? The water looked dark and murky but ahead I could see lanterns of bright lights, brighter than the midday sun. One part of me said, jump in the river, another part said, run. I turned and saw the most beautiful landscape, emerald green fields, majestic trees, flowers of every hue and form imaginable, birds and butterflies that I had never seen before. Such colours, such perfume, such music, such beauty, and such peace. I started running but my feet felt heavy, yet light at the same time. I wanted to sing with the music, but no sound would come. I was not afraid, although uncertain as to where I was going, or indeed, if I was going anywhere. There were magnificent winged creatures surrounding me, but there were no signposts, no sense of direction. I looked down at my dirty boots and said to myself, I don't belong in this beautiful land; I must go back to the dark river.

Bump, Crash, Boom! Someone was standing on my chest and burning irons into my side. I was coughing up blood.

I opened my eyes and found a sea of faces round the hospital bed. I recognised my mother, my two sisters, two of my cousins, my uncle and aunt, but there was a man's face close to mine, his tears dripping on to my shirt.

"Baba, Dad," I whispered. I wanted to shout but could not find my voice. I wanted to fling my arms around his neck, but could not find my arms. My father had come back to us. This was not a dream. It felt as if I had been on a long journey, but I had returned. Apparently, it had been two weeks, touch and go, they told me later. I don't remember anything, not even throwing the rock or being shot. The main thing was that Dad had come back and I had come back. Except for Fatima, we were a complete family again. I wanted to dance and skip for joy.

My right leg was covered in plaster and tied up in traction, fractured in two places. They told me I had climbed on to a low roof and when I was shot, I must have fallen into a pile of rubble. I don't remember anything, not even collecting the rock or climbing up and I certainly don't remember being shot. Apparently, they told me later that my leg could be fixed but it was my lungs they were worried about. A bullet had lodged itself near to my heart and one lung had collapsed. Somehow I had pulled through.

The doctors and nurses had been wonderful but I knew it was something or someone far more important than their care. God, for some unknown purpose had allowed me to live. I humbly acknowledged that I had been wrong. It was like groping in the dark for that elusive switch. I thanked God. Now I knew what I wanted to do. I wanted to be a doctor.

Four

The night air was heavy with the scent of honeysuckle and jasmine. The man in the Minaret was sounding out the evening call to prayer and Miriam sighed.

"Bedtime my darlings."

"Oh, Mama tell us a story."

As she tucked her two little daughters up she sang them a lullaby, just as her mother used to do for her.

> *'Close your eyes my sweet one*
> *Now the day is done.*
> *May God's mercy keep you*
> *Happy dreams come true.*
> *Sleep, sleep my lovelies,*
> *Sleep, sleep my lovelies'.*

They were her pride and joy except when they woke her up, wailing, in the middle of the night. Her firstborn, Lamia, now two, was just like her father: dark skin tight black curls, round cherubic face with rosy cheeks and long dark eyelashes. But Miriam could see something of her own disposition, that inquisitive energy and mischievous innocence.

The second daughter, Nivine, born a year later, was just beginning to toddle. She was fairer in countenance and seemed more delicate.

Amin always came in from the farm, tired and grubby, then he'd pick up his little girls, tickling them til they gurgled with delight and excitement. Miriam almost felt jealous. How come he no longer had time to pay her attention or tell her those wonderful folk stories, she thought. Then she would remind herself that she was no longer a child, but a married woman. Although he never mentioned again those magical words, 'I love you,' she knew he really cared.

She was often nostalgic for the carefree days of her childhood when she could run wild in the orchards and play with her friend Majida. How she missed Majida. She heard that she, too, had married and was living in the city.

Then her thoughts travelled back to the evening before her wedding day when all the women and girls of the village came to her Henna party. This was a traditional get together for them before the actual wedding. A huge straw tray, woven and dyed in different colours and full of flowers and herbs plucked from the garden, was carried high, with lumps of clay soaked in henna amongst the flowers. Miriam, amidst cheers and jubilation had to succumb to having her feet and hands painted with this dye. It had stained her hands for months afterwards.

Then the next day, the day of the wedding, after her elaborate make up was completed and dressed in her extravagant wedding gown, she had waited the arrival of Amin's mother, sisters and cousins to take her away from home. It was a time to be sad, so although she was excited and apprehensive she had to look sorrowful. Indeed her mother was silently crying. Meanwhile the rest of the women were dancing and singing, making up the songs as they danced, waving their scarves and handkerchiefs and wiggling their hips to the music.

'*God bless our beautiful bride,*

There is no one prettier,

Her brothers are handsome and industrious,

May God grant her many children.'

Then the bridegroom's relatives sang a similar song praising the virtues of the bridegroom.

'*There is no-one more handsome than Amin,*

No one more intelligent,

No one more hard working.

Amin, Amin!

You deserve this lovely bride!

God make him prosper

And give him many sons!'

It was like a competition between the two families as to who could extol the best virtues one against the other.

She remembered the monotonous rhythmic drumbeats of the music, the twirling of hips of the women dancing, their throat cries and monotone songs wishing Allah's blessing upon blessing on the young couple. Finally the bridegroom appeared, riding on a horse, while the bride and all her company had to walk the long distance to her future home, dancing and singing all the way. On arrival there was a big feast awaiting them, then a long line of congratulatory handshakes and gift exchanging, until everyone went quietly home.

She remembered the fluttering butterfly fear in her stomach as the family bid them goodnight and Amin led her into the bedroom. It was the first time she was to sleep in a proper bed, a stitched mattress stuffed with raw cotton on a wooden-slatted bedstead. She feasted her eyes on the beautiful blue quilted bedspread. 'How did they know my favourite colour? she mused. She had been used to a straw filled pallet on a rush floor mat. Amin had taken her by the hand and kissed her. He had been loving, gentle and patient, as she undressed, and for that she was grateful. She had since learnt that some men can be brutal on the wedding night.

Now she had two beautiful little girls. Amin loved them but would never be satisfied until she produced a son. Her own mother had had three boys before she was born. She constantly prayed silently that Allah would grant her a son next time.

"Day dreaming again," her mother-in-law said when she saw Miriam's face looking out into space and not paying attention to her chores.

"I was thinking, when the girls are older, I would like them to go to school,"

"Whatever for?" Um Amin said.

"Well, the world is moving on and nowadays it is important to know how to read and write. I wish I could read."

"Reading the news is for the men, we have enough to worry about without getting concerned about affairs of the country or government. They will tell us all we need to know," Um Amin continued.

"Aren't you worried with all the changes taking place? Remember how we used to have national celebrations in the summer when they had the big military parades and the bands playing loud music and everyone had a holiday. Well, we haven't seen the likes for two years now," Miriam declared.

"That's because there's a war on."

"Yes, I suppose so. But I used to love those little trips to Haifa, to watch the boats in the harbour, to see all the flags flying, the drummers beating the drums, the shining brass buttons on the uniforms and the black tassels bobbing up and down on each fez. It was all so exciting. Nothing ever happens these days. Life is so boring sometimes."

"You have your lovely little girls and we are enjoying so many good things," responded Um Amin.

It had been a busy day and Miriam was tired, but she had adjusted well to her new life. After all it was not so different to the kind of life she had as a child except that her mother-in-law, known as Um Amin, had replaced her mother as head of the household, and her husband had replaced her father's strict control. But Miriam still had that streak of restlessness and adventure. Nothing wrong in that most people would say but in her structured culture and with no education she felt stifled. She still had to do all the chores expected of her; collecting water, making dough and baking bread, preserving fruit, pickling olives, making cheese, drying herbs, etc. Her mother-in-law, whom she addressed as 'Auntie' was more relaxed and less dictatorial than her own mother. She was round, red faced and big bosomed. Her father-in-law was often sick with an asthmatic cough. He would just sit in his chair complaining, smoking his arguileh and expect to be waited on hand and foot.

The day always ended at dusk when the men would come in and expect all the food to be ready. Then Amin would sit with his father and brothers to discuss the farm business or other news, while Miriam had to be content to sit with her mother-in-law.

* * * *

One day, after a breakfast of goats milk cheese, olives and herbs with olive oil, the two women were relaxing playing with the children in the courtyard, when they saw some soldiers in uniform accompanied by two other official looking men walking down the path towards the house. The women gathered up their skirts and the two children and quickly disappeared into the kitchen, alerting Abu Amin and sending a message to Amin by one of his younger brothers.

Abu Amin was as usual sitting smoking his arguileh, so he stood up to welcome his visitors. He coughed and cleared his throat, then greeted them cordially and motioned them to sit down. Apart from the normal polite niceties of enquiring about his health and that of the family, they did not divulge their mission for some time. "I expect it's about collecting taxes," Um Amin whispered to Miriam.

Soon Amin appeared and told his wife to prepare lemonade first, coffee later. When the drinks were ready the women beckoned to him to fetch the tray, so that he would serve the men. Miriam, because custom decreed it, accepted the fact that women always had to stay in the shadows. Indeed it never occurred to her that the customs could change, but now there were all sorts of rumours going about that women were actually working alongside the men in the city. She just couldn't imagine it.

The men's voices seemed to rise and fall and at one point sounded angry and agitated but try hard as they could to listen, the women in the kitchen could only make out a few words. They were not words they wanted to hear: war, disaster, famine, and disease. They knew there was a war on and they had heard of many battles, soldiers being killed or struck down with plagues. They had heard of terrible fevers sweeping the country, of all the woodland trees being decimated to build railways for transporting army vehicles and equipment, of people leaving the cities to live in tents to avoid the cholera, of water becoming contaminated, of children going hungry…

But Um Amin and her family had not been overly concerned. They lived comfortably, had all the food they needed and so far had been protected from all these outside calamities. They did not understand why men should fight each other, why nations should make war against other nations, why there seemed to be so much hatred and suffering in the world. Why couldn't people live together in peace and harmony? Surely God was compassionate and merciful?

After the men had drunk coffee and what seemed like an interminable time of sitting and shouting, Amin and his father bade them farewell.

"Well, what was all that about?" Miriam was curious.

"No doubt, we shall find out in good time," Um Amin cautioned. It was best to wait for the information when the men were ready to talk.

Amin, his face dark with anger, his eyes red and bulging, swore and cursed. He put his hands through his hair and Miriam noticed that his shirt was wet with perspiration.

"Calm down son," his mother's voice broke the storm of fury, and Amin sat down while she brought him a cup of water. Miriam had never seen her husband so angry and upset. She suddenly found herself afraid of him. Abu Amin, meanwhile, although equally angry did not react quite so violently. He probably knew that life in general was fragile anyway and that he possibly would not live to see many more tragedies.

"You had better tell them what is going on," was all he managed to say, taking up his arguileh again and making huge puffs of smoke high into the air.

It was unusual to call a family meeting, although the men would sometimes discuss farm matters together. If it involved other families they would meet in the village square just outside the mosque or the church. But rarely, if ever, would women be included in decision making. Now, Amin was asking for a family meeting including his wife, his mother and his sisters. It must be serious.

It was late summer and the days were getting shorter. The harvest had been gathered in and it had been a fairly good year. They thanked God that they had enough provisions to last all the family through the winter with some to spare. The month of Ramadan had just finished but the three days of feasting afterwards had been more muted than usual because, as Amin said, they were lucky to have anything to eat at all. Amin had told them of the starving families in the city. He sometimes described the conditions of poverty and disease when he would return from his little trips. Any produce that he could not sell, he would give away. But he never talked that much about it so as not to upset them.

Miriam had fasted for Ramadan ever since she was a little girl, but at sunset when everyone would sit down to eat a big cooked meal spread out on a tablecloth covering the floor rug, she could forget her pangs of hunger. In fact during Ramadan, the women had more work, more cooking, more salads, more sweet cakes and syrupy pancakes to make than the rest of the year. It was also the time to invite relatives and friends to the evening breakfast. That was not the same as going hungry. What must it be like to have fasting day and night, she imagined. Unimaginable.

"It was nothing short of blackmail," Amin began.

"What does that mean," asked Miriam.

"It means being pressurised into doing something or else suffer the consequences.

Anyway, the army is desperate, so many are being killed or dying of disease".

"I have a feeling that the Ottoman government realise their beloved Empire is crumbling," Abu Amin butted in.

"What does that mean?"

"Just listen, will you."

Miriam decided it was best not to ask any more questions. It all sounded so official, and above her head.

"As I was saying before, people are dying of war and starvation. The soldiers said they would be coming back with a truck to empty our storeroom of grain, wheat, lentils, beans and anything else we have. We can only keep one sack of flour for bread. All must go, even the olive oil."

"Well, how much are they going to pay you?" This time it was Amin's mother to ask.

"That's the point, nothing, nothing at all. They said this is a new way of taxation.

They said it would be for the poor families, but I suspect it is to feed the poor army. Pure robbery is what I call it. They also wanted, Abdullah, my brother to join the army but I told them plainly no way." Amin's intense little speech had left him emotionally drained and everyone else had shocked looks on their faces.

Suddenly, his mood changed and he began to laugh.

"What's so funny, it all sounds like the end to me," his mother said. "Hurry, there is no time to lose," Amin declared. "The soldiers will be taking their afternoon nap now, but mark my words, they will be back before sundown. Mother find some old sheets, Miriam get out your sewing box. We are going to make some mattresses of grain and lentils!"

There followed a frenzy of unlawful but necessary activity, done in whispers, but with the children crying out of fear and confusion. In what seemed like no time at all, the noisy truck clattered down the muddy pathway into the courtyard, making the dogs howl and the hens scatter in all directions. It was Miriam's first encounter with a motor vehicle and for her it was nerve racking. She kept out of the way but watched from a distance as the soldiers loaded up the truck with sacks of grain and beans. One of the soldiers noticed a little trail of lentils leading into the house, so the soldiers demanded a complete search. The women froze with fear but fortunately for them Amin put on an air of coolness. Miriam, however, noticed his eyes were full of contempt and hatred.

"Welcome to our humble abode. You will see my wife has put some lentils in a tray for our meal tonight," then to Miriam, "Make us all some coffee."

It was Amin's apparent indifference and the coffee that had saved the day. The soldiers went away, never suspecting that some of their food stocks had been cleverly squirreled away in makeshift mattresses.

FIVE

"I'm afraid, Farres, we will have to do some surgery in your chest. We have located the bullet and according to the X-rays, we think there is a good chance that we can remove it without causing further damage to your lung. Then hopefully your lungs will recover and once your leg has healed, you will be back on your feet again in no time. We are giving you a course of new antibiotics, starting today."

The American doctor sat on my bed. I could tell he was a very tall man, not young but not old either. His greying hair was receding to reveal a wide forehead with a long straight nose making him look very distinguished. I studied his face and found it to be kind and honest. He continued to reassure me in English but I could only recognise a few words. However, the nurse explained what Dr. Griffiths had said and I nodded my head. Apparently, I had suffered concussion as well as everything else and my brain was still a bit fuzzy.

"Where is Baba? And Mama?" I muttered.

Did I dream that my father had come back? Or was I hallucinating? It can't really be true, surely. How was he able to get back into Lebanon?

"Your family have returned home, to the Shatila camp. You are in Beirut and very lucky to be here at all. The hospital in the Camp was shelled and burnt," the nurse said.

My mind was swirling with so many questions. How could I have been so foolish to get myself into this predicament? The consequences of anger. I remember feeling so impotent in the face of aggression. I had to do something. Why did the enemy always seem to win? Why was I too young to join any militia group? Why were refugees always treated as terrorists when they were the victims? Why couldn't I have been born in a peaceful country, like America for instance? What was this American doctor doing in a foreign hospital? Did he really care what happened to me? Why was my life worth any more than all the other young men who had lost their lives?

Anyway, the doctor seemed hopeful of my recovery and said I would soon be on my feet and my first thoughts were a determination to get well and strong again and then return home to take my school studies more seriously. I knew I had been lazy and not been doing my best at school. Consequently my grades were disappointing, but I had always blamed the war. School days were very erratic. In fact I couldn't remember the last time I was in a class.

But if my father has returned, will he take up arms again? He might get killed. Will the siege go on forever? Is my family being punished for my involvement? How much longer must we suffer the indignities and discriminatory injustices as Palestinian people? Will the day ever come when we can all go back to Palestine? As I lay in bed my brain was working overtime with questions…and more questions. The next morning the nurse said they had scheduled my operation for the following day. She handed me a scrappy piece of paper which brought tears of joy to my eyes. In Arabic I read:

'*To Farres. Get well soon son. We are all OK. We love you. Baba*'.

It was really true. My father had been at my bedside. He had come home.

It was several days after the surgery that I finally began to feel my strength returning. Every time I opened my eyes I was aware of lots of monitor tubes, drainage tubes and even to my acute embarrassment a tube and bag to collect my urine. A young nurse sat by my bed wearing a stiffly starched white apron. Her face under the starched cap was soft and tender. It was the prettiest face I had ever seen, large dark eyes, small, slightly upturned nose, and full lips. Her eyes were constantly on the monitor or checking my appearance. Her smile touched my heart!

"What's your name?" I ventured.

"Vicky," she said.

"Vicky, talk to me. Tell me about your family."

"Well, my father was killed in the war and our house was bombed but not completely destroyed. We have managed to patch it up."

"Mother, brothers and sisters?" I asked.

"I have one sister, older than me. She works in an office. My two brothers are still in school. My mother is often ill, so my sister and I have to work to keep all the family. I am training to become a nurse."

"Wow, so your family have suffered too?"

"Yes, my grandparents came to Lebanon from Palestine in 1948."

"My great-grandmother also came here to Lebanon in 1948. You don't live in a refugee camp?"

"No, we had relatives here from before and so we are able to live in Beirut, although when my grandparents first arrived with their parents, they had to live in a refugee camp like everyone else. Also the church helped us to settle here."

I was not sure what to ask or say next. I was not too friendly with Christians. "You know the Christian Phalagists murdered my sister."

"Oh, I am so sorry. We are not those kind of Christians. Of course I heard about the massacre and we condemned what they did." She apologised again and said she had to leave me for a while to attend to other patients.

I had a lot to think about but I had a lot of company to talk to. There were seven other men in the ward, four beds on either side. Some of them were young men who had been wounded like myself, but some were old men with beards who were always groaning and shouting for the nurse. I was the youngest. I learned, too that they were all different religions or factions, who, had they been well and on their feet would have been shooting each other. Lebanon was such a mixture, Shiite Muslims, Sunni Muslims, Maronite Christians, Orthodox Christians, Druze, Armenian and some who didn't fit into any of those categories. I admired the doctors and nurses who gave the same care to all.

Every morning the junior doctor who had long hair tied back, greeted us. He wore a white coat that often looked as if he had been sitting about in it all night. He said he was 'neutral' and didn't believe in any religion or faction. We knew this couldn't be true, as he spoke Arabic like the rest of us. It was obvious he did not want to arouse any political passions. He was kind and gentle but the way he spoke was something else!

"Bloody miracle, you are," he greeted me, laughing. "Your angels must have been working overtime...or were they little devils?"

Everyone laughed.

"He's the little devil," my next-bed companion shouted out loud.

"And now he's fallen in love with your Nurse Vicky," another man joined in.

"Well, well, well, bit young for that kind of mischief, aren't you, Farres?"

I blushed crimson and tried to hide my face under the sheet. Had I said something about Vicky to my neighbour? I must have remarked on how pretty she is. The whole ward was laughing, some of the men clutching their stitched up stomachs. Worse was to come. Next time Vicky came into our ward, the men whistled.

"Your lover boy, Farres wants to see you."

"Aw, go on the lot of you. Be nice to the poor lad," she said.

Then she came over to my bed and plumped up my pillows to make me more comfortable.

"Don't mind them," she said to me.

"I really...do...like you," I whispered.

She planted a light kiss on my forehead and I was in heaven.

Every morning the doctors did a ward round, often with a group of young medical students discussing my case. That was the part I didn't like. They would turn down the sheet and examine my body as if it belonged to someone else. Some of them didn't even look at my face. I was just another statistic. Years later when I, too, was a student doctor I reminded myself constantly to look at each case as a human personality. The senior doctors were different. They addressed me cheerfully with:

"Good morning Farres. And how are you today?"

The hospital was not immune to the war. There was often the sound of exploding bombs and the distant echoing cracking of gunfire. Beirut was still being shelled and bombed, people still being killed or maimed, the different factions still sniping at each other. Foreigners were being taken hostage; suicide bombers were blowing up government buildings and foreign armies were interfering. We heard news on the radio daily but it was difficult to tell the truth from the propaganda. What a mad world we live in, I mused.

After weeks in hospital with all the attention, care and good food, there was a part of me that almost dreaded going home again. It seemed much safer and certainly more comfortable than my family home in the Camp. I had to admit also that I enjoyed the joviality and teasing of the other patients. Most of them were cheerful, trying to hide their pain. But there had been dark moments too, like one evening when Mustapha, one of my bed-pals had been fiddling around in his locker, collecting up his bits and pieces into a plastic bag because the doctor had told him he was due to be discharged the next day. He suddenly collapsed on the floor and died. The nurses quickly put a screen around his bed and later he was carried off to the mortuary. This was the man who had been more cheerful than the rest and had been particularly helpful and friendly to me. He told me that he had a son my age so I reminded him of his boy. We were never told by the medical staff why he had died so suddenly. Was it a brain haemorrhage or a heart attack? It seemed so sad that he was ready to go home when it happened. It certainly sobered all of us. There was no talking for the next twenty-four hours. It also made me realise that I was no longer a child. I had become a man.

The day of my discharge arrived. Nurse Vicky and the others came to say goodbye. I realised that I would probably never see them again. But had I not grown-up? I steeled myself not to cry, as Vicky put her arms round my shoulders.

The Red Cross ambulance transported me and another patient back to Shatila. I was able to take with me some items of food such as tins of sardines, a sack of rice and a large bag of beans. As we drove through the streets, I looked out through the tiny scratched gaps in the darkened windows of the ambulance and viewed scenes of destruction. Tall apartment buildings were listing sideways with their facades blown off, some of the beds, tables and chairs covered in concrete slabs were perilously hanging over the edge, shop-signs dangling upside-down by wires, shards of glass everywhere, traffic lights blinking, while half destroyed, smouldering fires and burnt out cars and the piles of rotting vegetables on smashed market stalls were visible on each corner.

When we reached the gate of the Camp, the military guards did not want to let us through but after searching the vehicle thoroughly and arguing over the papers, they finally conceded. As we entered the Camp, it was not the destruction or piles of dirty rubbish that struck me. I had seen it all before. It was the smells. I had become familiar with the antiseptic hospital smells. Now my nose was invaded with the stink of stale blood and urine and the stench of open sewers.

I suppose I had imagined a welcome party but then I realised that every family was mourning the loss of someone either through war or starvation. My own family, though, gave me a tumultuous welcome. I walked into my home and marvelled that I had found my feet again, but I was emotionally exhausted with all the hugs and kisses! I looked at my father again, whom I had not seen since the day I emerged from my coma in the hospital. He looked older and thinner. His eyebrows and moustache looked bushier and there were new creases in his brow and on his cheeks, but his smile, unique from anyone else, was the same.

"Baba, how did you get back into Lebanon?"

"I'll tell you all about it one day, son."

I insisted. "No, I want to know, now, Baba."

It was a question I had asked myself a hundred times.

"Well, to cut a long story short, I came by ship from Tunis to Syria, then disguised myself as a Syrian fighter.

"Wow, that was brave," I said. "What was life like in Tunis?"

"It was good on the whole. The people were friendly and welcoming and we were free to move around. We were well looked after and had good jobs, but all the time I was homesick for my family. It's so good to be back even though I can see there is still so much suffering. I knew

53

you wanted to join the resistance, Farres, but thank God you are still alive. It seems I came just in time, now we can start all over again," he said. I didn't dare ask him what he meant. Did he mean that he and I were both going to fight again or did he mean that we would just start again as a family?

"It will soon be your birthday, Farres. Sixteen, almost a man, we must celebrate," said Mama, making light of the situation.

Suddenly, my emotions spilled over. I was crying like a baby. Sixteen? I had tried to act like a man amongst the men in the hospital and now my mother was saying I was not quite a man yet! I had to admit that I had a lot of growing up to do yet. My mother was so wise.

Six

Majida, as every day, looked out from her balcony. She loved to watch the tides come and go, and contemplate how the mood of the sea seemed to match human moods. One day the sea would be green, dull and still, another time it would be wild, the waves crashing against the rocks, white foam sprayed high into the air. Today it was a perfect blue, mirroring the sky, with a million tiny diamonds dancing on the waves. It made her feel that today was going to be a good day.

It had not been easy, at first, to adjust to city life, and sometimes she felt homesick for the slower rural pace of her hillside village and the more temperate climate. Haifa was so hot and sticky, she could never quite get used to the humid heat. Her husband, Yousif, kept a shop downstairs, and worked from early morning till late at night, selling all sorts of household goods. There were knick-knacks, hard and soft brooms, candles, walking sticks, tobacco pipes, lamps, buckets, small stools with woven cane seats, coffee pots, trinkets, arguilehs, storage jars, etc. etc. The list was endless.

His business was prospering now that the Turks had left and the British were in control. The British soldiers did much of their shopping with him and he was always friendly and obliging. If he didn't stock what they were looking for, he would obtain it by some means or other. Also the British were not used to bartering, so they paid whatever price he asked, though Yousif was an honest man, which was more than could be said for some of the Arabs, or so was the unfounded but popular belief.

Yousif was doing well and Majida was happy to be provided for, with her family of three girls and a boy. The two eldest girls went to an elementary school in the city and Majida enjoyed the little walk every morning to take them to school, but sometimes, when she was busy with the baby she allowed the girl who helped her occasionally to take them. Her boy was only six months old. He was a beautiful baby. She was especially protective of him because her first son had died, a victim of an epidemic plaguing the city when they first arrived. Now, this new baby had been named Issa in memory of her little brother who had drowned in the well.

By chance, one morning, Amin walked into the shop and recognised Majida with the baby in her arms. "Aren't you Majida, Miriam's friend?" he said.

"Yes," replied Majida. Her face flushed with embarrassment, but also immense joy as she realised who he was.

Amin turned to Yousif and stretched out his hand. "My name is Amin Kassem. So you are…"

"Yousif, Abu Issa (father of Issa), husband of Majida. Welcome, welcome. How wonderful to meet you."

Majida could not contain her excitement. "Tell me, how is Miriam? I do miss her. It seems such a long time. We were such good friends when we were growing up in the village."

"Miriam is fine. We have three girls and a boy. His name is Tha'er, so I am Abu Tha'er".

"Same as me, three girls and a baby boy", Majida exclaimed. There was so much she wanted to know. How she longed to see her childhood friend. It would be so wonderful to connect again.

Amin sensed her excitement. He remembered Majida and her family coming to their wedding but somehow they had lost contact over the years.

"I must bring Majida to Haifa to meet you again," he said.

"Oh, that would be lovely."

Amin was given coffee and almost forgot what he came into the shop for, but the two men became engrossed in a deep conversation, not just about family and finance but politics too.

Majida quietly slipped away upstairs because the baby had started clamouring for her breast.

"How's business these days?" asked Amin.

"Very good, my best customers are the British, so I have been trying to learn more English. What about you? How's the farm?"

"Fine. I recently bought a few sheep. Their milk makes good cheese. Have you tried it?"

"Yes, it's great. Maybe you can find something in the shop to help with your kitchen equipment."

"Oh, I guess we're a bit old-fashioned. We do everything by hand".

"Yes, but that's a lot of work for your wife."

"True, I suppose…anyway, one day maybe…"

"Take a look."

Amin went around the shop seeing so many things piled up on shelves and buckets hanging on hooks, and he was reminded of a funny story.

"I must tell you this funny story," he looked across at Yousif.

"Go on".

A poor man with a wife and ten children
had only one room to sleep, cook, and live in.

He went to the Mayor to ask for more land to extend his dwelling. The Mayor suggested that he add a parrot in a cage. But, the man said, how can I find room? Just do as I say, said the Mayor. After a week the man came back crying. I have even less room now, what shall I do? The Mayor told him to put a donkey in the house. How will I find room for a donkey? Just do what I say, said the Mayor. This went on for several weeks when the poor man was desperate, tearing his hair out. He now had a parrot, a donkey, some chickens and a sheep, all sharing his one room with his wife and ten kids.

"I can't bear it any longer", he screamed.

Finally, the Mayor said: "Now go home, take out the sheep and come back after a week to report to me".

The poor man did as he was told and reported back that things were still bad.

So the Mayor said, "This time take out the donkey".

The man returned again after a week to report that the situation was a little better.

The mayor again gave his advice to let out the chickens and the parrot.

The poor man went home, did as he was told and soon became very happy!

Yousif and Amin fell about laughing.

"That's a good story with a good moral. It has a political meaning too," said Yousif.

"Oh, I'm not into politics," said Amin.

"You should join our Christian-Muslim Association and hear our prominent speakers," effused Yousif.

"Ah, but I don't know enough about it and besides, I am always too busy on the farm."

"Well, come and watch the protest demonstrations we are planning at the end of the month," continued Yousif.

"What good will that do?" declared Amin.

"We have to make a show of Arab unity."

"We are united, aren't we?"

"Not exactly, there is a lot of division, these days."

"Is it true what I've heard that we will become part of Syria?" asked Amin.

"No, I don't think so, the Zionists are getting stronger."

"But the British support the Arabs, don't they?"

"We can't be sure about that. I've heard that the British Government is sympathetic to the Jews."

"No, that's not possible, the Arab leaders will not allow it. I've heard that the British are appointing Palestinian heads of local government, judges, and a new body of Muslim religious dignitaries in Jerusalem."

"Mark my words, this is all temporary. You do not live near the harbour as we do. We see boatloads of Jewish immigrants arriving every day…"

Yousif then started to rummage in a pile of newspapers and periodicals, pulling out an Arabic newspaper printed a few days before.

"Look here," he said to Amin. "Can you read?"

"Of course, I can read."

"Well, the front page, as you see, is all about local news in Haifa, new business ventures, the new factory soon to be opened, market prices, etc, but look inside you will find some foreign news that is terrible. There are ghastly things happening that we don't hear about."

Amin scanned the paper but did not fully understand it.

"Abu Issa, you read it to me. I learned to read at school, but the Arabic words here don't make much sense to me."

"OK, I'll read it to you."

Yousif proceeded to read several paragraphs from the newspaper. It described terrible events of massacres and starving orphan children in other countries. It even told of whole populations being transferred from one country to another, in exchange for other large communities, because of religious differences.

"Maybe we will have to suffer similar tragedies."

"I never heard about all these terrible happenings. I had no idea." Amin was visually shocked. "I don't believe such things can happen here."

"We hope not but we should demonstrate and support our Arab leaders," said Yousif. "It's frightening, but quite honestly I am afraid to get involved. I don't want to get my family in a dangerous situation".

"Of course not. I guess I am over-reacting. After all, we are enjoying a fairly peaceful time at the moment. The British always treat us well, and as Muslims and Christians we are united in Palestine, aren't we?"

"Yes, of course, we are. Let us talk about happier things. Now I came to buy some new lamps…"

After looking around the shop again and finding what he needed, Amin paid and prepared to leave. For friendship sake, Yousif had given him a generous discount.

"You will stay for lunch, won't you," said Yousif.

"No, I must be getting home, I have taken up too much of your time already," Amin politely replied.

"Oh, but I insist, you must have lunch with us", then calling up to Majida: "Um Issa, lay another place for Abu Tha'er". The Arab custom was that it was more polite to address a person by naming their first born son.

Yousif closed the shop and the two went upstairs to find a feast of chicken, rice, vegetables, with cheeses, olives, salads and fresh fruit. After lunch they started discussing the arrangements for the baby's baptism which was planned for the following Sunday. It was at the suggestion of Majida that Amin and Miriam be invited to the baptism. Majida remembered what she had told her friend after her little brother's funeral.

"I told your wife at the time: you are Miriam, the Mother of Jesus, and my brother's name was Issa, which means Jesus. That's why we have called our son, Issa. Miriam and I are 'sisters'," she declared.

Amin laughed nervously, taken aback by all this effusive hospitality and gestures of friendship. He did not know how he could refuse but was flummoxed because he had never been inside a church before. Yousif sensed the problem and assured him that other Muslim friends would be present and it would be a good opportunity for the two 'sisters' to be reunited.

So Amin returned to the village very happy and when he told his wife she was overjoyed.

* * * *

Sunday arrived. Amin and Miriam prepared to make the short trip to Haifa by donkey and cart. They filled a large basket full of fresh fruit as a gift and Miriam had knitted a little baby jacket. She dressed up in her best dress, black linen with red and gold elaborate embroidery on the bodice and down the sides and hem of the skirt. She then wore her special fringed shawl over her head and numerous gold bracelets on her arms. Her mother-in-law was not too happy being left with the three girls, but Miriam took her baby boy, Tha'er with her.

Miriam couldn't wait to see her friend. She was so flustered and agitated with excitement as she prepared for the journey that Amin became impatient with her. "Why all this fuss? We are not going far."

He liked Majida and Yousif a lot, but was also nervous about going to a church. The journey was uneventful except that Miriam was again told off for talking too much.

The reunion was more wonderful than even she had anticipated. The two women hugged and kissed, their tears flowing unchecked, then they both stood back, looked at each other and laughed. They had so much to talk about. They compared the two babies, Issa and Tha'er. Tha'er was actually about five months older than Issa, almost a toddler. He was also much darker and his eyes were larger. The two men sat and drank coffee while Miriam helped her friend prepare the lunch.

They giggled like the children they once were.

"My dear, dear sister, how I've missed you."

"Me, too, how I love you." declared Majida.

The baptismal service was bewildering for the Muslim family yet they found it beautiful. There were so many pictures in the church. In fact the walls were covered with paintings of the Virgin Mary, different saints and a big picture of St. George. This was in strong contrast to the interiors of mosques, which avoid images of every kind. They were also conscious of a strong smell of incense and scented candles.

At the entrance, the old priest, with his long white beard, took the baby in his arms, chanting words that were incomprehensible. Then the godparents took the child, stripped him of his clothes and handed him back to the priest, who was girded with a large towel. The priest then dipped him into the stone bath-like font three times. "In the name of the Father, the Son and the Holy Ghost." All present chorused the Amen.

Issa came up out of the water gasping for breath, then bawled his head off, which everyone took to be a sign of a long healthy life. He was soon comforted by his many relatives, who wrapped him quickly in a towel and then dressed him in new white clothes. Everyone was given candles to hold, which they lit, from person to person. The family walked around the front of the church three times, chanting songs, above the noise and clamour of the many children who were now running around freely. Meanwhile, Majida, the mother of the baby, stood quietly to one side. She was not allowed to hold her son until the ceremony was over.

As for Miriam and Amin, they observed everything quietly. It was all very strange. However, everyone was welcoming and friendly, so they enjoyed being there. A reception followed, in a little room next to the sanctuary where cakes and sweets were served. When they were preparing to leave, Yousif handed Amin a string of glass beads. They were green-blue in colour, reminding him of the sea.

"Worry beads," he said, laughing. "To stop you worrying, Amin!"

It had been a truly wonderful day.

SEVEN

_____

The coming winter months were cruel and harsh and the Amal Shi'a Militiamen were crueller than the weather, to the point of being ruthless. Had they no heart? I thought. Were we not all fellow Muslims as well as human beings?

There had been a few months of respite since the summer ended with a cease-fire, but with the onset of winter another siege began which turned out to be longer and more traumatic than the first. In between, all the people of the Camp had been frantically busy building up defences, digging tunnels and trenches, finding new ways to smuggle in arms and ammunition, making underground shelters clean and secure, and above all organising committees to unify the whole population. They initiated a form of rationing food so that people could share, making sure that there were stocks of flour for the bakery and dried milk for the children.

My father was, inevitably, very involved in the committee organisation. He roped in the women to thoroughly clean out the shelters and disinfect the public toilets, which also involved putting down a growing population of rats. Then he found some secret storerooms to hoard sacks of flour. We could not live without bread and one of the first things our enemy did was to burn down the bakery. Children were also busy, helping in the digging of tunnels, some of which had to be done after nightfall. I joined in with the digging, even though my leg was still not too strong. Sometimes I helped carry planks of wood to reinforce the tunnels, but this was back breaking work.

There were even committees for burying the dead, which Baba was also involved in. Anyone killed in battle was a martyr and was buried quickly, preferably at night and sometimes without any prayers because being martyrs we reckoned they had already gained favour with God. Mama and I were very relieved to hear my father promise that he was not going to be involved in any fighting, though he was often in danger because of collecting casualties.

After two months in hospital I had returned to see our home in a different light. It was as if I had changed glasses although I never wore them. A while after the euphoric welcome and celebration I looked around and noticed the changes. The concrete floor had a few small mats, several mattresses piled up in the corner, and a couple of upholstered cushions. Our one and only cupboard was deprived of its doors.

"Where has our sitting room chair gone? Where are the cupboard doors? Where have the shelves gone?" I said.

"Oh, Farres, dear, you see our *kanoon*; we have no charcoal to burn in it. We are going to freeze to death this winter, so we had to chop up the furniture to store for firewood," my mother said.

I was shocked. Then I learnt that water was almost non-existent and that we had to take buckets to collect rainwater from pools, filling up the bomb craters. The Amal had constantly shelled the water pipes but the Palestinian people were just as determined to repair them, and repair them they did, many times over. But when we had to resort to rain water, it meant boiling it in large pans over the wood stove. No electricity either, which although we had been used to going without for some time, my father found it very hard. When he was deported abroad he could watch the news on television. Any electricity was saved for the medical clinics.

I wanted to check out my shoebox. I was relieved to find it was still in the back of the cupboard with my little inherited 'treasures' from Granny Miriam intact.

"What on earth do you want with that rubbish?" my sister Farida said.

"It's not rubbish. Granny told me to keep them safe."

"Dirty garbage," she said, making rude faces at me. "Of course, if there was a speck of gold, we could sell them, but these things are worthless,"

She snatched the box out of my hands and ran to the door.

"Don't you dare…" I screamed at her.

"What will you do if I tip them all into a mud hole", she teased, laughing.

I suddenly became angry and grabbed her by her long hair.

"I'll kill you," I said.

"Now, now, what's all this about. Farida, leave him alone and Farres, no more of your temper tantrums, please."

My father had interfered, probably wisely, but to me it was a blow to my pride. I realised I was no longer the master of the house and no longer could I boss my sisters around.

Then, one morning, I found my mother sitting on a little stool in the kitchen. She had just vomited in the latrine and now she was weeping, her hands over her face as if to hide her tears from the family. She was really quite distraught. I put my arms round her and tried to comfort her thinking it was just the strain of trying to feed the family and run the household. She shivered violently so I threw a blanket around her shoulders.

"Oh Farres," she said. "What shall I do?"

"What is it Mama?"

"I think there is another baby on the way. Your father wants another son but I don't have enough strength".

Normally, I should have said 'Congratulations,' but I suddenly felt even more resentful that my father had come back. I made up my mind not to show my feelings.

"Well, Mama, we will look after you and try to bring you food. You must get strong again." The situation was still far from normal with daily curfews and restrictions.

When the news broke that my mother was pregnant, everyone said "Congratulations," but I could tell by the looks on their faces that their happy wishes were not entirely genuine. Their concern for her, though, was very genuine. They realised my mother was frail, having gone without proper food herself in order to make sure her children had enough to eat. The little local shop had completely run out of food stock, the only things left on the shelves being a few household cleaning materials and light bulbs and what use were those when there was no electricity?

We heard that some families had sent out their womenfolk and children on food missions, escaping over dirt tracks and sand hills to reach grocery stores outside the Camp. It was a very risky business. Some women had been shot dead on these dangerous short trips.

"Mama, mama, don't worry, I will go outside the camp and get some food". My younger sister, Fayrouz, aged ten, was volunteering to go with her cousin Randa about the same age. Surely the soldiers would not shoot two little girls. They set out at dawn the next day wearing old coats and headscarves, and cautiously picked their way through thick mud and rocks until they came to a small gap in the barbed-wire fence. They carefully squeezed through, and ran along the main road as fast as they could, eventually sitting down by the roadside to catch their breath.

All we could do was sit nervously and wait. At dusk, we spied two little figures in the distance trundling along a very dilapidated baby pram with two wheels missing. Some of us went out to help them the last few yards and they fell into their mothers' arms utterly exhausted. They had been out all day but had achieved their mission. Inside the pram were cartons of dried milk, bags of sugar, tins of corned beef and tomato puree and even a bag of candy, which they said was a gift from the shopkeeper.

"We were scared to death, until we were far away from the Camp," they said.

"Where did you find the pram," I asked.

"Oh, it was in the corner of a bombed out building, but it was full of bricks. I think the workmen were using it as a wheelbarrow, so they must have wondered where it went. We had to tip out the bricks first."

We laughed and praised them for their bravery, saying "*Al hamdulillah*, Thank God", over and over again. What a celebration we had that night, in spite of the noisy shelling around us.

Several weeks later my father asked me to run down to the medical clinic that had been set up locally as a temporary surgery. It was the only place to treat patients as we could not reach the hospital in the other Camp next to us.

"Your mother is not well. She needs to see a doctor. Also your sister Fayrouz is sick. She needs medicine."

"What's the matter", I asked.

"I can't say for sure but your mother is bleeding a little and has cramps. Your sister has diarrhoea and vomiting".

"I'll get a doctor," I said, pulling on my jacket and rushing out into the rain.

The clinic was teeming with people of all ages. I couldn't move. What a sight of deprived humanity. While a young woman was trying desperately to register the names of the patients and give them cards, the patients were just as desperately clamouring for attention. They sat in rows on long, low wooden benches; bent old men with long cassock-like robes and white keffiyehs, women in various stages of pregnancy with swollen bellies, trying to control toddlers clinging to their skirts or running around wild. There were young men in ragged jeans and jackets waiting for their wounds to be redressed and amputees in wheelchairs or hobbling on crutches. Some were trying to make a joke of their condition, denying the pain, while others were cursing angrily. The makeshift clinic consisted of two large rooms, probably once two ground floor apartments merged into one with the partitioning walls knocked down to create more space, so there was very little privacy. The walls had been whitewashed but were inevitably soiled with grubby finger marks, graffiti and blood spatters. Had I not been in a modern hospital I would probably never had noticed all these deprivations.

I tried to shout above the clamour of babies crying but it was impossible to get the attention of any of the medical staff. Then an English doctor spied me. Apparently he had remembered me from the time when I was shot, but of course, being unconscious, I didn't remember him.

"Farres," he shouted, "just a minute."

He pushed his way through the crowd and put out his hand.

"Tom Jones...not the singer," he said, laughing. "I suppose you don't remember me, Farres."

"No, I don't, Doctor."

"Well, I remember you very well," he said. "You almost died when you were shot. I managed to get you to the hospital in Beirut." His blond hair was thick and untidy and his white coat spattered with blood, but his blue eyes and wide mouth gave me the broadest smile ever.

"You saved my life." I stuttered.

He brushed aside my compliments and thanks.

"All in a day's work," he said. Then his brow creased. "You were lucky. Two other boys were killed that same day. Anyway, how can I help you now?"

"My mother and my sister are both ill at home." I explained the problem.

"Give me an hour and I will come and see. Meanwhile, give this medicine to your sister. Tell her to take two tablets immediately." He fished out a packet of tablets from his pocket. I was so relieved that I had not had to wait too long, like some of those other poor people.

That was the beginning of what became a warm friendship with Dr. Tom Jones. I was anxious to learn more from him about how he managed to get me to the hospital, when two other boys had died. My mother must have been distraught thinking I was dead. I must somehow make it up to her and now that she is ill I will do all I can to be helpful. I know I am no angel and have caused my family a lot of heartache.

I ran home to give Fayrouz the medicine and waited for Dr. Tom to appear. By the time he did come my mother was getting worse. It was obvious that nothing could be done to save the baby, but at least she did not need an operation. Dr. Tom gave her some tonics and told her to rest in bed a few days. Then he ordered her to have some blood tests. My father was particularly upset and was so worried. He felt she should be in hospital but that was not possible under the present circumstances.

Before Dr. Tom left, I had a word with him. "Doctor," I said. "I don't know how we can repay you for saving my life and for all your attention to my family. But I want you to know that I would like to study medicine one day and perhaps save the lives of others."

"Farres," he said. "first of all you must call me Tom. If you like, you can come after school and help us in the Clinic. We are always in need of volunteers. Perhaps you can help me learn some Arabic, too."

"I would love that," I said, trying to sound not too exuberant in case I failed. "I will do my best to come whenever there is no school."

School classes were still very erratic because of the war and the constant danger, but as often as I could I went along to the Clinic. It was pretty scary and upsetting at times, but on the whole I enjoyed it. I learned how to roll bandages, how to take pulses and temperatures and how to explain to the patients the instructions for taking their medicines. They even gave me a white coat to wear which made me feel very grand. But life in the clinic was sometimes very chaotic trying to control the unruly children, helping young mothers when they started screaming out of fear, having to deal with mopping up messes of vomit from the floor and holding my nose at the smells. My experience of hospital had taught me a lot about bodily functions! I also learnt a lot of English while Dr.Tom, as I called him, (it seemed disrespectful to call him just Tom) learnt many Arabic phrases from me.

When my mother's blood tests came back from the laboratory we were all very concerned because it meant that she had a severe blood disease which could not be treated by medicine.

EIGHT

Miriam already a middle-aged matron now, with a much rounder figure, still possessed that same abundant energy and inquisitive nature. She knew it was no good asking her husband questions. He used to get irritated and impatient by her curiosity in everything including other people's affairs, though he knew in his heart that Miriam was very intelligent and frustrated by her lack of education. He appreciated her efficient way she handled the affairs of the home and farm. Even she was keeping the accounts in order. Tha'er had taught her how to write simple Arabic words and figures and how to do sums. But she could not read. The written Arabic of books and newspapers was a different language to the every-day spoken Arabic.

It was a glorious sunny day in May and the purple and crimson bougainvillea was stunning against the newly whitewashed walls of the house. Miriam was picking fresh vine leaves to stuff with lamb meat and rice for dinner.

"Mama, can I talk to you a moment?" Tha'er looked worried.

"Of course, my dear, what is it?"

They sat down on stools under the vine, Miriam piling the leaves into a fold of her skirt.

"I want to get married."

"Why, that's great! Congratulations! We have been waiting a long time for this news. You are already twenty-four and your father was married at sixteen!"

"Yes, I know, Mama, but I was waiting until I could save up enough money."

"Well, who is the lucky girl?"

"This might be a problem. She is a city girl from Haifa whom I met while in College.

"O Tha'er, what about your cousin Rania. You know your Aunt was expecting you to marry her daughter".

Tha'er groaned. "I know Mama, I like Rania a lot but I am in love with Sawsan. She is from a good Muslim family. Her father works for the British Army."

"No, no, your father will not approve. You know very well that it won't work. It is better to marry within the family or at least within the clan."

"But, Mama, now people are saying it is not good to marry one's cousin."

"Who says? What nonsense. It's always worked for us. Besides, this Sawsan, if she is a city girl she will not want to come here to live in a village."

"No, Mama, we want to rent a small house in Haifa."

"What? And how do you think you can afford that?"

"Well, I have a good job as accountant and Sawsan has a job as clerk in the same firm."

This was not only incomprehensible but also shocking to Miriam. For her eldest son not to bring his wife home, for her to be working and in the same company. What was the world coming to! She had always looked forward to being a mother-in law and teaching her daughter-in-law how to cook and look after babies, just as her mother-in-law had taught her. She was devastated.

"We are in love, Mama."

"In love? That's disgusting! Love comes only after marriage."

The conversation was beginning to turn into a heated argument and Miriam decided to leave it. She felt hurt. Although she had always been in favour of new horizons, she was not ready to accept new concepts of traditional customs.

"Well, talk to your father. I have things to do," she said, walking away.

Miriam had borne ten children all together, although two, a girl and a boy, had died in infancy. Her three daughters, born before Tha'er, had all married and had children. They lived in the village so were close at hand. Then there were two more sons and two daughters. The other sons, Mahmoud and Mahfouz helped on the farm and were much more compliant. They, too, were planning to marry soon but within the 'clan.' Tha'er had always been a bit of a rebel, adventurous, confident and self-reliant. It was the same restless spirit that his mother had as a young woman, the difference being, of course, that Tha'er had had the advantage and privilege of a good education.

Amin came home; humming a popular song loudly and looking very pleased with himself.

"Guess what?" he shouted, not addressing anyone in particular. Miriam was sitting at the table rolling the last of the stuffed grape leaves.

"What?"

"I've bought a car."

"You've what?"

"I've bought a car," Amin repeated. Yousif is teaching me to drive so I've left it in Haifa now but soon I will bring it home".

"I don't believe it," was all she could say. Two big shocks in one day. She couldn't spoil all the excitement and enthusiasm of Amin's happiness by telling him about Tha'er. She began to wonder now if Amin might accept the news in a more positive light. She decided not to say anything. Let Tha'er tell him, she thought.

The family were all jumping up and down hugging their father and congratulating him. "That's great," Miriam eventually joined in but saved her hugs for later. "We shall be able to visit Yousif and Majida more often," said Amin, and for Miriam that was the best news ever.

Yousif had bought a second-hand car over a year before and had since been trying to persuade Amin to buy one. Finally Amin had given in when one day Yousif had pushed him into the driving seat of his own car and showed him the controls. It wasn't so difficult after all, he discovered. Yousif was also still trying to get Amin involved in the political scene and although Amin was sympathetic with the motives he was afraid to get implicated.

About two weeks later, there was a loud clatter and clanking interspersed with short snorts. The family all gathered at the door to watch. Miriam compared it to a wild animal hell bent but pausing to break wind. They looked again, in astonishment, as not one, or two but three cars appeared. In the driver's seat of the first one was Amin looking flushed and proud but dripping with sweat. Yousif was sitting beside him. He stopped just short of the gate, jerked on the brake and wrenched open the door.

"Bravo, bravo, well done," shouted his family.

The second car was driven by Issa, ready to take his father home. The third car was left at the top of the lane and five strange men started walking slowly down the path. They were all dressed very smartly in western style suits, shirts and ties. Only the older man wore a red fez.

"These are Sawsan's relatives," whispered Amin to Miriam as she hurriedly disappeared. It seemed Tha'er had invited them to meet his folks and to arrange a day when the men of the family could go and officially ask the hand of the bride. Miriam did not come out to greet them nor was she allowed to be present at the *tulbeh,* the official asking of the bride's hand, so she did not actually meet Sawsan until the engagement two months later. She had imagined a tall, lanky, sophisticated girl when in fact she had a pleasant surprise. Sawsan turned out to be petite, fair-skinned, pretty, reserved and very, very sweet.

* * * *

HAIFA 1945

"Take us for a walk, Grandma."

"By the sea. We want to see the ships."

"OK, but be good children and hold my hands."

Majida thought no sooner have I reared my seven children, than here I am looking after my grandchildren. Issa's twin boys were delightful companions and she really enjoyed taking them to the harbour. They were jumping up and down with excitement. The sea seemed calm and another big ship was disgorging its passengers and cargo. Jewish refugee immigrants as usual. The British had tried to limit the number of ships arriving with refugees from Europe, but still they continued to come every day. Thousands of them. The Arabs were getting nervous to see so many, building farm settlements and communal kibbutzim. "Soon they will outnumber us," they said.

The British, too, were nervous. Zionist terrorist gangs were already attacking hotels and buildings where the British worked, trying to persuade them to leave Palestine. Yousif had foreseen this happening years before but nobody believed him. Majida, though, felt really sorry for the immigrants. She had heard that the war in Europe was over and that these were survivors of terrible catastrophes. They called it the Holocaust. She could hardly believe that such evil men as Hitler could massacre millions of human beings.

"Who are all those poor people, Grandma?"

"Why are they carrying things in bundles?"

"Why do they look so sad?"

There were old men with gaunt tired faces, some with beards, looking like they were near the end of the road, yet obviously not so old in age. Women carrying their possessions in an old blanket or sheet tied up with a bit of string, their faces thin and pale, their heads covered in scarves or small hats. Children crying and clinging to their mothers with eyes that looked either too big for their faces or sunken in. Only a few of the younger generation were smiling and waving to the crowd awaiting them on the docks. Most had no one to welcome them.

There was a sense of pathos that these people who had suffered so much were now nervously and anxiously ready to start a new life. They had been told that this was a land of freedom, a land without people, a land that God had given them. They were returning to God's land just as the Hebrew exiles came home from Babylon all those thousands of years before. Yes, although they had never set foot on Palestine before, they were coming home!

Majida was hanging on to the twins when a sudden squall blew up. The waves were leaping up the sides of the harbour and the wind lifted up her skirt. Her hat blew away tumbling down the walkway. She tried to hold her skirt down, run after her hat and hang on to the twins. "Hold on to my skirt, both of you", she shouted, as the hat disappeared. She stood looking at it and wondered what to do next.

"Is this your hat?" Majida turned to face a young woman with a little boy, about five or six years old. "Oh, yes, thank you," she said. The woman was trying to remember some English, which neither of them knew very well.

"I need help", she said, her eyes looking straight into Majida's eyes and her hands folded together in front of her face as if pleading for mercy. The twins stared at the little boy who had no shoes on and only ragged shorts and a thin shirt. The boy started to cry. He wasn't sure why these two well-dressed boys were staring at him. His mother spoke sharply to him in a foreign language. Then the woman took hold of Majida's arm. Her ragged clothes stank of sweat.

"I…go…with you…home".

Majida didn't know what to do. It would have been rude and unchristian to shake the woman off. Without a word, she started for home, hoping that Yousif would be able to deal with the situation. They entered the shop and Yousif was busy serving customers, but seeing his wife's face he sensed the problem. She gave the woman and her son two stools to sit on and beckoned the twins to go upstairs.

Yousif had learned a few words of Hebrew so between Hebrew and English they managed to communicate.

"Just one room with water…I pay rent," the woman pleaded.

"Why don't you go to a kibbutz with all the other people?" said Yousif.

"Because, in kibbutz they take my boy away," she said.

"Where have you come from?" asked Yousif.

"Poland. All my family perished. Father, mother, brothers, sisters, husband and…baby." She started to weep.

"How did you escape?"

"Long story…" she sighed deeply and Yousif thought it best not to probe further.

As it happened there was a small room at the back of the shop with a yard, and a gate. There was a latrine and a water tap with a bucket. Yousif showed her the room and Majida brought down some old mats, a few cushions and blankets. She also made sandwiches for them, which were very gratefully received. The boy was ravenous.

"Oh, and what is your name…and the boy's?"

"Rebecca, my son is Vadivich, call him Vic."

"Poor, poor people", said Majida as they shut up the shop and went upstairs.

The day had not ended, however, before two men came banging on the shop door. When Yousif opened the door and courteously invited them in, they refused to enter but started to talk to him angrily. By their dress and little caps perched on the backs of their heads, Yousif knew they were Jews.

"Can I serve you anything?" said Yousif.

"No, we have come to enquire about a Jewish woman and her son who we believe you have hiding in your home?" One of the men spoke accusingly.

"It is true I have given refuge to a Jewish immigrant woman, because she pleaded with us. I am certainly not hiding her from the authorities." Yousif tried to sound polite but he was also angry. To think that these gentlemen were accusing him of what they considered to be a crime. "It was her choice," added Yousif.

"Well, she has to come with us. There are special centres set up for refugees and immigrants."

"Come with me", said Yousif.

They followed him into the shop and into the little room at the back. They found Rebecca and her son curled up together with blankets, fast asleep. It was a rude awakening but she quickly gathered up her few things and carrying the boy followed the men out without a word. As she was leaving, she turned to thank Yousif with a look of sadness on her face. Although Yousif felt sorry for her, he was glad to be relieved of the responsibility of her welfare.

NINE

Tha'er's plans for his wedding were not going as smoothly as he had hoped. At least he had found a nice little house in Haifa, and his brothers had helped in whitewashing the interior walls and cleaning it out. He was anxious to get married quickly but there were problems. Since his father was always too busy to talk to, he once again turned to his mother. Fortunately, after meeting Sawsan, Miriam was now in agreement with the marriage and had gladly accepted her new daughter-in-law, though was still disappointed that they would not be living with her.

"Mama, what shall I do?" Tha'er asked.

"Now, what's the problem?" Miriam answered, putting her embroidery down.

"Well, it's a bit embarrassing really."

"What is?"

"You see, Sawsan's parents like me, but since they have met you and Baba they are not so sure."

"Why, what do you mean?"

"They consider themselves to be in a class above us. We are just peasant farmers. They belong to the city elite".

"What! I never heard such nonsense."

"Maybe, if you wore a more modern dress to the wedding?" Tha'er was embarrassed.

"Certainly not! I shall wear my new *filaheh* dress. It is much more elegant than their western-style suits."

"I agree Mama."

"What's more, Yousif and Majida are city people now, Christians too, but they are not snobbish. In fact Majida was a village girl like me." Miriam was indignant.

"But there is another problem."

"What's that?" Miriam was anxious to get on with her work. She couldn't believe what she was hearing. Too high and mighty for her wonderful son, eh!

"The family are thinking of emigrating," continued Tha'er.

"What do you mean? Leaving the country? Why? Where to?"

"They say war is imminent and inevitable. Sawsan's father has been given a British passport since he had an important post working for the British. He can get a job in London."

"That's ridiculous. Leaving Palestine! If there is a war, all the Arabs will come to our defence."

"That's not what Sawsan's parents say. They are sure the Arabs will be defeated and the Zionists will take over the country, but God only knows what that will mean for us. We just hope we can continue as we are. Anyway, they are thinking about leaving."

"Poor Sawsan, she will be left behind, I suppose."

"No, that's the point, they want her to break our engagement and for her to travel with them." Tha'er looked so downcast, he was almost in tears.

"Oh, that's terrible. What does Sawsan want?"

"She wants to stay with me. We are not afraid."

"Then you must both get married as soon as possible. Next week will be the olive harvest and it will be all hands to the pump, as they say. After that we must not delay."

"Oh Mama, thank you for being so understanding."

Miriam rolled down her sleeve and took the tip of the hem to wipe Tha'er's tears. She gave him a big hug, as if he was her little boy all over again.

October was always a busy month with the olive harvest, but this year it was a bumper harvest. The trees were literally weighed down with the plump black olives, and so it was 'all hands to the pump' as Miriam had described. Neighbours were helping neighbours. When one set of trees had been picked, there were more trees waiting. Then there was the task of putting them in sacks and taking them to the village press to extract the olive oil from some of the fruit and pickling the rest. It was hard work but also happy work. Since the women had no time to prepare cooked meals they all picnicked under the trees. It was great fun. And there was enough olive oil to last two years.

Everyone was talking about war. Every day the news was full of violent incidents. Arabs ambushing buses full of Jews, holding them up in the middle of the road, then killing the occupants. Jews were placing bombs in Arab markets and throwing grenades into Arab houses. But they were also attacking the British, urging them to leave earlier than planned. Meanwhile the Palestinians were hopeful that the Arab armies of Syria, Jordan, Egypt, Iraq and Lebanon would come to their aid. They did not realize that although the combined troops of Arab armies were about equal in number to the Zionist armed forces they lacked the training, discipline and motivation, besides not being as heavily armed as the Jews. No one disputed the fact that the Jews were highly sophisticated in manpower and military affairs. Moreover they had the backing of the World Zionist Organisation.

It was in this atmosphere of fear, panic and uncertainty that Tha'er arranged his wedding in the village with the cooperation of the local Sheikh. They hired the village hall and all went off without a hitch. Sawsan looked like a princess and reluctantly all her family attended. Yousif and Majida were, of course, also invited with their family. Issa, already married with twin boys, had become a close friend of Tha'er, just as his parents were close to Issa's parents. The whole village joined in the festivity which, for a time, at least, managed to ease some of the tension and stress.

Meanwhile Haifa docks became a flurry of activity, with so many families leaving. Sawsan refused to believe that her parents were actually going to London. Newly married to the man she loved, it should have been a time of intense happiness and she couldn't bear the thought of her mother leaving for what seemed to her the other side of the world. She daily went to see her parents to try to persuade them to stay but her father was anxious to leave, not just for the sake of a good job and a more peaceful life but he was thinking too of his son's future, Sawsan's brother, and worried that he might get caught up in the fighting. She watched her mother pack boxes and boxes of articles for the journey including a big trunk to hold all the clothes. They gave Sawsan some of the furniture and the rest was sold. It was only when she saw the vans loading up stuff to be sold that Sawsan came to realise that their departure was inevitable.

On the day, Sawsan's mother was dressed up in all her finery, long ankle-length coat in an iridescent peacock blue with a high frilled collar. She had abandoned her usual Islamic headscarf for a large brimmed floppy hat with only a few wisps of hair showing. Sawsan was grief stricken but her mother tried to hide her emotions. Amin and Miriam stood on the quayside with them looking out of place in their village dress but Miriam did not feel inferior. On the contrary she stood straight and proud. Her son was as good as their son, she thought. As they all waved goodbye, Sawsan buried her face in her husband's chest while her parents and brother walked up the gangway to the ship. Crowds of other people were doing the same, porters scurrying up and down the gangway carrying the luggage.

"We'll be back soon," they shouted, but everyone knew that was too optimistic. Tha'er did his best to comfort his new bride but for some time she felt really lost. Then before the new year dawned, she discovered that a baby was on the way.

As winter approached, the city was beginning to empty of its population. It was the richer, more educated people who were leaving, fearful of being caught up in a war. Even some of the schools were closing because there were no longer any teachers. Some of the Arab organisations were encouraging people to leave, others were demanding, even insisting with threats that it was imperative to stay. Hence there was so much confusion and panic that most people didn't know what to do. The poor people, of course, had no option but to stay. So while there were ships arriving at the harbour bringing Jews from all over the world, there were also ships taking away Palestinians, some to Arab countries, some to the West.

Yousif was caught up in many political discussions and spent his time in the men's club talking about these matters. Majida began to get frustrated.

"Do you have to go to the Club tonight, dear?"

"Yes, tonight we have a very important meeting. We have to try and sort out all this confusion."

"Please don't be long. I get lonely sometimes."

"I promise. I will come home as quickly as possible".

Majida had always had someone to keep her company. With all her children married and living in different parts of the city, Majida felt lonely.

As soon as Yousif had locked up the shop and gone to his meeting, some troubles erupted. Majida sitting alone in her home over the shop, could hear the sound of gunfire and the sirens of British police cars. At first it was in the distance then the sound of explosives became louder and nearer. "O Lord", she prayed "Bring Yousif home safely". She did not fear for her own safety. Unbeknown to her, of course, the British soldiers had entered the clubhouse and arrested Yousif, ...'on suspicion of subversive political activity with possible plans of violence'. It was a terrible mistake. Yousif had no intention of engaging in any political violence. He only enjoyed the friendly arguments and discussion of political opinions. Never in his dreams would he be party to anything involving the arms struggle. No, Yousif was a peaceful man. Had he not shown kindness and given hospitality to a poor Jewish refugee?

As the evening wore on and Yousif did not return home, Majida started to really be alarmed. She started to imagine all the terrible things that could have happened to him, but she could do nothing but sit and wait. Suddenly she heard noises in the shop and then a peculiar smell. She opened the door leading to the top of the stairs and saw the shop was engulfed in smoke. It all happened so quickly. Some said afterwards that it was a firebomb thrown through the window, others said a spark from somewhere had ignited the fire, but within minutes the whole building was in flames. What with all the brooms, stools and piles of other wooden articles plus bottles of kerosene for the lamps, it was easy fuel for an inferno.

Majida tried to reach the balcony but the iron railings were too high to climb over and she was soon overcome with the acrid fumes.

She lost consciousness quickly. They later found her body completely incinerated.

Meanwhile, Yousif, after interrogation, was set free to go home. He found a big crowd had gathered in the street. For him, there was no shop, no home and worst of all, no wife. His sons and daughters were all standing outside and were surprised to see him arrive. They had concluded that he, too, had perished in the fire. They all clung to each other, too shocked to speak or even weep. The firemen had managed to save neighbouring property but nothing was left of Yousif's shop.

Meanwhile in the village, Miriam was up early, as usual, sweeping out the courtyard and tut-tutting to herself about the mess the menfolk had left behind the evening before. They did nothing but talk and smoke and chew watermelon seeds. The yard was littered with cigarette butts and shells of seeds. A neighbour ran into the yard giving her the terrible news about the fire in Haifa, but at first she did not realise the full implications. She called Amin to find out more details and he came back quickly hardly knowing how to break the news to his wife.

She was standing in the kitchen preparing the breakfast when she heard about her 'sister' Majida. Her knees buckled and she managed to collapse onto a chair. She was overcome with grief, burying her head in her lap and weeping inconsolably. Her sister, dead, how could that be? An hour later and she was still sitting, unable to move, when Amin came in to tell her to get ready to go to the funeral.

"My legs won't hold me up," she cried.

"Come on we must go," Amin shouted, "One of the workers will drive the car."

She was reminded of the sad funeral of Majida's little brother in the village church when they were both children. Now they were attending another Christian funeral but this time in a big city church. Indeed the packed church showed how much Majida had been loved and respected in the community.

Would this be the end of their close relationship, she wondered. As it turned out, the families were drawn closer together, especially the two sons, Tha'er and Issa. Issa had been helping his father in the shop, now he had to try to set up his own business, and take his father into his own home. It was some time before Yousif could come to terms with the fact that within minutes his whole world had disappeared. Little did he realise that before too long the family losses would be far greater.

TEN

HAIFA 1948.

Yousif sat up in bed with a start, the sweat pouring down his nightshift, his beard all matted and his hands knotted in fear, the blue veins standing out like a complex of angry rivulets. Five months had passed since Majida's death but he had not shaved since that day and the constant nightmares and self recriminations had aged him to the point when he became more and more withdrawn from his family. He kept asking himself why had he left Majida alone and gone to that meeting. Nothing had been achieved anyway. It was all talk, talk, talk.

The only spark of joy that kept him from losing his mind completely was the love of his twin grandsons. They would sit, one on each knee, vying with each other for attention.

"Granddad tell us a story."

"Tell us about the time when you were a little boy."

Sometimes he tried to relax and hugging the little ones to his chest, he related tales of happier times in the village.

"There were no noisy motor-cars then," he would say, "only donkeys and horses."

But sometimes he was too tense to even think about the past. It was the future everyone was worrying about now.

There had been a big storm the night before, black clouds had made the sea angry, the waves pounding the rocks, the thunder echoing around the mountains and the sharp electric lightning cutting the sky up into divisions, followed by torrential rain. Nothing unusual in an April storm. It happened every year signalling the end of winter, but the people of Haifa felt it was an omen of bigger storms to come. And they were not talking of natural storms. It was as if God in His heavens was sounding out the drumbeats of war and catastrophes.

Although trying to force smiles and an air of normality, everyone was terrified. There had been weeks of explosions set off by Jewish forces in Arab neighbourhoods as well as sniper fire in various districts. No one was brave enough to even go shopping unless it was for essential food. On top of that there had been talk of massacres in some of the villages, notably news had been announced on the radio and loudspeakers that hundreds of men, women and children were gunned down in a village just outside Jerusalem. The Jews were actually bragging about it, congratulating the perpetrators of these massacres and using them as propaganda to terrorise all Palestinians. "Unless you leave now, the same thing will happen to you," was the battle cry heard over and over.

By mid April, the residents of Haifa were leaving in droves, lorries of all kinds lining up to transport them to God knows where, hoping against hope that this was just a temporary measure and that when the situation had calmed down or the war had blown over, they would be allowed back. " No point in packing up completely," they said. "Let us just take a bundle of clothes for the journey and some staple foods like rice and tinned milk for the children."

A couple of men were designated to each lorry, hauling up the women and children who could not climb up on their own. It was bedlam, the children crying out of fear, the young women clutching their babies to their breasts and the older men and women who could not stand like cattle in the truck, squatting in the corners covering their faces and trying to shut their ears and eyes to all the clamour. Also ships had come to the harbour to transport the people north and those who didn't get on the lorries were herded onto the ships. They couldn't take any luggage with them and most people were quickly forced onto the ships with just the clothes they were wearing. There was panic and a sense that there was no time to lose and no time to even think about what might happen if they stayed.

Tha'er had sent word to Issa to say that they had returned to the village and inviting Issa and his family to follow. Issa didn't know what to do. Should he get into a truck with his family and travel north? Or should he try to go south to the village of Al-Tira where Amin and Miriam lived in their idyllic farmhouse? There was no time to mess around; the Jewish soldiers were in every street, knocking on every door. "Leave everything and go," they said.

An elderly couple just down the road had refused to move. "We are not leaving, this has always been our home and here we are going to stay. We'd rather die than run away."

"Right," said the officer, "if you'd rather die, then you shall die," and with that the poor couple were shot dead on the spot. It added to the fear and panic of the rest of the street.

Some were leaving by sea, but not in the big ships but in little private boats. A friend of Yousif's who was a fisherman filled up his boat with supplies and ushered his family aboard. Unfortunately, the boat was overloaded and capsized, drowning most of the occupants.

Issa decided to take the car south to the village. He started cranking up the engine, turning the handle round and round until it finally spluttered into life, at first fits and starts, then a gentle purring sound, much to Issa's relief.

"Get in, all of you, and be quick before the engine dies again. We may only have enough fuel to get us to the village."

Issa's wife, Lucy, was short and plump, very young with a full bust, ruddy cheeks and a shock of light brown curly hair. She had a happy disposition and was well organised. She had tied up various bits of clothing and bedding into an old sheet which Issa helped her secure to the roof of the car. In the front sat Yousif hunched over, then in the back Lucy, the children and Lucy's younger sister. Once out of the city, they sought out the quiet country dirt tracks to avoid the main roads. Some trucks passed them going in the opposite direction. "You're going the wrong way," people shouted.

It was uphill most of the way but the little car managed to transport it's precious cargo all the way, even though there were times when they had to get out and push it to dislodge it from the mud ruts. After all the rain, the ground was soft and muddy in places but it was wonderful to smell the fresh earth and the new green leaves and shoots.

Finally on reaching the village, there were some Arab soldiers guarding the entrance but they did not prevent the family from driving ahead. Amin's farmhouse was now two storeyed and it seemed like an oasis of peace and calm.

"Welcome, welcome, welcome. Thank God for your safe arrival". Amin and Miriam, Tha'er and Sawsan, and all the family were waiting with outstretched arms to welcome the travellers from Haifa. Miriam, overcome with emotion, wept on Issa's shoulder. "You are my son, now," she said.

It was truly a peaceful oasis with a more temperate climate than Haifa and without the constant noise of traffic and war. In fact, apart from calls to prayer at regular intervals from the nearby village mosque, the only noises were the cooing of doves, the crowing of the dawn cocks and the friendly voices of animals and humans on the farm.

Miriam was in her element. She loved, more than anything, to be surrounded by people, the more the merrier. It was like the old days when all her children were young. She had plenty of family around her now and her tongue was wagging, chattering and gossiping all day long. She did not mind at all that the little farmhouse was bursting at the seams. Amin, too, was happy to have a constant audience to laugh at his jokes, and he loved taking the children around. For them, it was a whole new world with so many new discoveries to be made each day.

Yes, for Dan and Sam, the twins, it was their first encounter with animals. They were both fascinated and delighted as they were introduced to the chickens, the sheep, the goats, the dogs and the donkey. Their constant exclamations of "Look, Uncle," opened up the eyes of the adults to things they had taken for granted all their lives. They were given a small basket each and shown how to collect the eggs every morning. It became a competition as to which one would collect the most eggs, until in their eagerness they dropped and cracked some of the eggs, which put an end to their little game.

"Look, Uncle, look," they shouted one day. "Why are those ducklings following the chicken?"

Amin laughed. It really did look comical. The brown hen was strutting ahead, proud as punch, with a brood of tiny ducklings following her.

"It seems Mama duck left her eggs, so the hen took over and sat on them till they hatched, so she thinks the ducklings are her babies." The boys giggled.

There was a small pond where the rest of the ducks lived and the twins spent hours just watching all the pond life of fish, tadpoles and tiny insects. They also became friends with the two dogs that would nuzzle their wet noses in their eager little faces.

Even Yousif emerged somewhat from his sad depressive mood. He sat contentedly in the courtyard watching all the comings and goings and contemplating the simple goodness and honesty of these friends. He knew there were some in the village who could not understand the complete openness and family inclusiveness of Muslims and Christians living together but those were obviously bigoted, religious people. Yousif was religious, too, in his own way. He loved the church and all it stood for, the ceremonies and their symbolism and clung to his firm faith in Christ which had been Majida's too. But now Miriam was claiming Issa as her son as if it had been ordained! It was Majida who had put the idea into her head. Mary and Jesus. And now Majida was dead. Yet, Yousif knew that Miriam was not trying to convert Issa to her own religion. Yes, now that he no longer had any responsibilities of home or shop he had time to sit and think. Sometimes the deep thoughts would trouble him and the nightmares make him afraid.

Meanwhile, Issa, although not used to country living, found himself helping in all sorts of ways, even milking the goats and making the cheese. Everyone was so happy they were almost afraid to voice their inquietude. They did not want to break the spell by pessimism.

Yet, deep down they knew that this paradise could not last forever. It was too good to be true. Besides, the news coming to the village was all very distressing. Most of the nearby villages had been evacuated, the occupants having either fled in fear or forced out of their homes at gunpoint. Also they heard that the British had packed up and left the country, the Arab armies defeated except in some areas, and worst of all, only a month after leaving Haifa, the country had become a new state called the State of Israel, a country with Zionist aims of a Jewish population only. As for the British, they were no longer their trusted friends; they had become hated traitors.

Miriam's family worries were the marriage of her two younger sons, Mahmoud and Mahfouz, and the safe delivery of Sawsan's baby which was due in July. Amin advised his sons to get married right away even if it meant without a celebration. They had both planned to wait until after the summer harvest and unbeknown to his family Mahfouz had been quietly stashing away cash over a considerable period, hiding it in a large handkerchief in a crevice of the wall inside the house. He hoped to soon have enough money to start building his own house, so he was not in any hurry to get married now. The house must come first, he said.

Mahmoud decided to take his father's advise and so in early June the family had a quiet wedding celebration and Mahmoud brought his new bride to the home. Another space had to be found for the couple, another mouth to feed, but Miriam was happy to have a new daughter-in-law.

By this time many of their friends had left the village including two of Miriam's married daughters and their families. She had not had word from them since. Sawsan was also worried that she had not had a letter from her parents since they left the country, but then nothing in the way of post or communications was functioning properly.

So far Sawsan's pregnancy seemed to be progressing without problems, but she was getting very tired and by July everyone was getting very jittery. What if they should be forced out before the end of July? What if the baby did not arrive before then? What would happen to all the farm animals...and the grain to be harvested?

It was a miracle that this hillside village of Al-Tira, so near to Haifa, had still been left in peace after three months since the evacuation of the city. The people knew that peace could not last. They had few arms to defend themselves, no Arab army to rescue them. But everyone went about their daily tasks, hoping against hope that they would be left alone. Everyone was holding their breath.

Eleven

"You see," said Dr. Tom one morning, as we sat sipping small glasses of hot sweet tea, "your mother's body factory has gone on strike. It is no longer making sufficient new red and white blood cells to keep her well."

Dr. Tom had a way of putting across human biology that made it sound so ordinary and simple yet so interesting and complicated. I was learning such a lot. When he had extra time we would sit in one of the tiny offices in the clinic and discuss the treatment of some of the regular patients or basic anatomy. We often needed one of the nurses to translate.

"Factory?" I asked. "Where is the body factory?" The word factory conjured up images of dozens of little men in blue overalls working on machines with tools, or rolls and rolls of fabric being made up into items of clothing.

"Ah," he said. "I was waiting for you to ask that. The blood factory is in the middle of your bones." He smiled, waiting for my reaction of utter surprise.

"Wow, you mean to say that our blood depends on our bones?"

"Yes, everything in our body depends on another part working properly. The blood depends on the bones, the bones cannot work without muscles, the muscles cannot work without nerves, the nerves cannot work without the brain, everything needs the blood to nourish it and the blood needs the heart to take it around the body." Dr. Tom gave me some books to read but they were in English so I had to borrow a dictionary to use all the time.

"Wow," I said. "What a lot I have to learn, but thank-you for all your help Dr. Tom."

"You will make a good doctor, Farres, if you are determined and dedicated to study hard. Maybe, one day I will try and help you to get to England to study seriously. But don't get your hopes up too high."

"That would be wonderful," I said.

The spring sunshine was warming our homes and our hearts and drying up the mud roads. The siege had finally ended, but everyone was too exhausted to celebrate. The last thing I remember was when all the women had organised themselves into a big demonstration for not being allowed out of the camp by the Amal soldiers. I thought they were all very brave, especially when it brought back memories of my sister going on a similar demonstration and they were all murdered by Lebanese Christians and Israelis. Then the next thing was the lorries and trucks of food supplies coming in and everyone making a mad scramble for the sacks of flour and rice and tins of dried milk.

Mama became weaker and weaker, until, in spite of herself, she had to take to her bed. We took it in turns to sit by her bedside and hold her hand until the end came in the middle of the night and she passed away peacefully in her sleep. It was a sad time for all the family and over the next few days many friends came to condole us. My mother had been so kind and unselfish to everyone. I never saw her lose her temper or say an unkind word. I would never forget her, but relieved in a way that her suffering was not prolonged.

I went back to school and we all had a lot to catch up on. My uncle and his family managed to patch up their home and returned to live upstairs, but my aunt would often come down to help my sisters prepare the food.

Meanwhile my father managed to get a job doing some repairs to property and he was also busy on various committees organising the general running and defence of the Camp. But in the evenings, he would often open up to me and tell me something of the Palestinian exile of 1948 and other historical events. He was born that year so he could only tell me what his parents and Granny had told him. Of course, in school we learned all about Palestine, refusing to call the land by its new name of Israel.

One Friday morning, when Baba had gone to pray at the mosque, Farida came to me with a serious look on her face.

"Farres," she said, "We have to look for a new wife for Baba. You know a man needs a woman,"

"You mean you need someone to take over the cooking and cleaning?"

"No, silly. All men need a woman to share their bed."

"Well, no one can take the place of Mama."

"But Baba is still young. I can see it in his face. He is frustrated and unsettled."

"How would you know what men need. It is only six months since Mama died."

"I tell you, Farres, we have to find him a new woman."

"What, us find him someone? Let him look himself!"

"You know that's not possible. He has no sisters, so it's up to us. Anyway, I know your sneaky ways. You have been eyeing that girl down the road. I've been watching you."

"No, I've not."

"Yes, you have, you have .." her mischievous look and taunting fingers withered me and made me blush.

"You're blushing. Farres is blushing!" she chanted, loud enough to make her little sister come running.

"I'll get you one of these days," I said, giving her threatening looks. "I'll wring your neck."

I ran out of the door and almost bumped into my uncle.

"What's all the noise about?" he said, going up the stairs.

"Oh nothing, nothing." I began to feel guilty. Farida had come to me with what she had decided was a serious problem, but I had not taken her seriously and now she was accusing me of something, which I had to admit was true. But I was certainly not going to admit it to Farida or anyone else for that matter. On the spur of the moment, I decided to follow my uncle upstairs.

"Hang on, wait for me," I shouted.

My uncle turned round. "Coming to visit us, are you?"

"Yes, I want a word with auntie, if it's possible?"

"Sure, come in."

Auntie Leila, as we called her, was doing some laundry in the kitchen. She wiped her hands when she saw me. "Why, Farres, what a pleasant surprise!" Auntie Leila was always in our house but it was rare for me to go upstairs to hers.

She was treating me like an unexpected guest and I didn't know quite how to react. "Don't mind me," I said. "Continue with what you are doing. I just thought I would pop in."

"Farres, there is something on your mind. Did you quarrel with your sisters? I know you are missing your Mama too much."

I felt a lump rise up in my throat but told myself I must not cry. I am a man now.

"Just going out again. I forgot to buy cigarettes." My uncle seemed embarrassed, so I was glad he left.

Auntie Leila sat down with me alone. The children were all playing outside.

"How are you?" I said, trying to make conversation.

Auntie Leila looked at my face and sensed my emotional battle. "Let the tears flow, Farres," she said. "It is not unmanly to cry."

She hugged me as I sobbed. It was not just missing Mama, I knew. It was my pride and guilt at being so selfish and unfriendly to my sisters, it was my longing to be free like a bird, it was my frustration in trying to study hard with so few books to help me, it was my lack of confidence and hope in the future. What chance was there ever of breaking free from this prison-like camp. My father may want a new bride but would he be happy afterwards? He had tasted life outside. He would still be frustrated in this Camp with no decent jobs and no civil rights. Although he had manual work, it was really not his scene. He was intelligent and very good at organising. His activities in the committees were all voluntary so that would not pay the bills. My thoughts were running away...

I dried my eyes, while Auntie went to fetch me a glass of lemonade.

"I am worried about Baba," I finally managed to blurt out.

"Why, what's the matter."

"Farida said he needs a wife. She said he is unsettled and nervous."

"Umm, maybe. What do you want me to do?"

"Baba, doesn't have any sisters and doesn't seem close to any of his cousins. His only brother died, so he has no one. You are Mama's sister-in-law, so I thought you could help find someone?"

"Well, let me think about it. Come and see me in a few days time". I was a bit surprised that she had taken me so seriously. She was so kind to us when Mama was sick and I really warmed to her. I knew that she did not have an easy life with my uncle. I did not tell Farida anything immediately but later on I just said to her that aunt Leila was going to fix everything. She gave me a look of condescending surprise.

Meanwhile, it was true that I did have my eye on a very pretty girl, who happened to be the sister of my school-friend Mohammed, the boy who was not so rough with me when I trespassed on the hiding place of the lads who had guns. I had only spoken to her briefly, once at Mohammed's house and discovered her name was Amal. We spoke about her name because it had so many bad connotations. It means 'Hope' but it was also the name of the militia who had been so cruel to us all.

Anyway, I knew I could not get involved with any girl seriously because I must put my career first and there was no future of any career in medicine if I stayed in Shatila. My only hope was to get away. I guess I was putting too much hope in Dr. Tom and here I was falling for Hope. It was all so ironic. Anyway, I had two more years at school, but there was no harm in dreaming.

Aunt Leila said she was still trying to figure out a solution to our problem. I say it was our problem, though it was really my father's problem even though he hadn't been consulted. One day Aunt Leila invited me upstairs to meet her younger sister, Lamia, who was a teacher in the Girls School. She was what one would describe as plain looking, but very friendly.

Actually, she was Fayrouz's class teacher. We talked about school and lessons and other general matters but avoided any mention of my father. But I knew why she was visiting. It was now the business of my uncle to make the suggestion to my father. A date was arranged when my father and Lamia would be left alone together to talk things over. It seemed they liked each other and Lamia already in her late twenties was anxious to get settled down to married life. There was not much of a life for a single girl in Arab society, especially in a refugee camp.

There were problems, of course. My father couldn't afford much gold or an expensive wedding celebration. He would have to borrow money to pay for basic gold bracelets and rings without which her family would not agree to the marriage. For Lamia, she was concerned that she would lose her freedom to continue teaching, which she loved and was also a bit worried that she did not know much about cooking. But the plusses outweighed the problems. Baba would be happier and we would have a new mother. He agreed that she could continue teaching until a new baby arrived and her sister Leila would teach her how to cook. The outcome of all of this was a happy engagement, the couple deciding to wait until after the first anniversary of Mama's death before the wedding. Naturally the engagement party was muted with just close relatives and no singing or dancing. It was therefore a surprise to hear loud music on the street outside. We looked at each other. "What is going on?" we all declared in unison.

There was the distinctive noise of bagpipes and drums with a crowd of children and others singing songs and waving flags. I stood at the door and watched as a whole group of them passed by our house joyfully chanting in Arabic:

> *Palestine I will give you my years,*
> *I will sacrifice my life*
> *Your sun will rise despite the massacres,*
> *The chains and the oppressors.*
> *Palestine I ask myself*
> *As the tears choke me*
> *Why does the child have to die so young?*
> *For us his memory will live forever.*

They were celebrating the beginning of the 'intifada' or uprising in the Palestinian territories on the West Bank. It was for our Palestinian brethren the beginning of a period of great hardship and suffering but all we could do in Shatila was listen to the news and follow the events without being directly involved. They were protesting the Israeli occupation and they thought by confronting the army with stones this would alert the world to the injustices and ultimately lead to a peaceful settlement and maybe…just maybe…justice for the refugees.

Twelve

NORTHERN PALESTINE 1948

Mid-July and the day had been hotter than usual. Some of the family were sitting outside in the cool air listening to the sounds of the dark. The grasshoppers were chirping merrily and the mosquitoes were buzzing around their heads annoyingly but it was the owls hooting to each other that disturbed their thoughts. They hardly dared speak about it for the sound of the owl or *'boom'* surely meant doom. "I feel it is the end of the world. We must repent," declared Yousif. Normally the others would have scoffed or even laughed at him but they kept silent, each one with their own dreadful thoughts of fear and panic, wondering what the morning would bring. There had been the distinct noise of gunfire for several days and word had got around that some of the Arab guards at the entrance to the village had been killed. That only meant one thing. There would be no one to defend them and the Jews would take over just as they had all the surrounding villages. They had every cause to be alarmed.

"Perhaps we had best get some sleep before the end of the world," said Amin.

Nobody laughed.

If any of them slept, it was fitfully at best. Some members of the household couldn't even shut their eyes. Only the slumber of the innocent belonged to the children but even they were awakened around four in the morning with the loud barking of dogs. Suddenly there was a deafening boom.

"Is that thunder or..." Miriam cried.

"No, it is not thunder, it has to be an explosion somewhere," someone answered.

The men put their heads out of the door to see clouds of smoke coming from a building nearby but what alarmed them most was the sight of soldiers, carrying lights and guns, marching down the hill towards them.

"Oh my God!" Amin's face showed signs of terror, even though it was still not daylight and no lamps had been lit. Quickly, he alerted everyone, locked the door with a huge metal key and tried to barricade it with a large wooden trunk, which held many of their personal possessions.

"Miriam, quick, put some food provisions in a basket, they are coming for us."

Issa and his family had seen it all before. They had already fled from Haifa three months before. They waited, uncertain what to do next but the women quickly dressed, putting on two or three dresses on top of each other as Amin had instructed them beforehand. The men were already dressed, having slept in their day clothes, the city men in suits but Amin and his sons in their traditional long coat gowns over wide pantaloons. The children, conscious of the adults fear, were terrified, crying and clinging to their mother Lucy, while she was doing her best to calm them.

The next sound was shouting and screaming coming from the neighbours' house and then the dreaded moment arrived. The soldiers were hammering on the door shouting in Arabic but with a foreign accent "*Iftah,* open the door." Lucy almost suffocated the kids with her hands over their mouths, while everyone else stopped breathing.

"Open up, or we'll burn the house down!" followed by several shots of gunfire in the air.

"Please open Amin. I couldn't bear the sight of another fire," pleaded Yousif. The memories of his wife's incinerated body and his burnt down shop and home were still haunting him. Mahmoud and Mahfouz moved the trunk away and opened up the door.

"You'd better all go quietly. We need to search the house for weapons," the officer even sounded polite, but other soldiers were deliberately pointing their guns at them.

"Can we come back after you have searched?" Tha'er pretended to be naïve.

"We will see, but you have to leave the village right now."

The sun was beginning to rise, as the mist covering the hills rose also, leaving a wonderful glow in the sky. Each new day they had always woken with thankful hearts to God for the beauty of the earth and sky, but it seemed that God was absent today.

"You are a big family"! one of the soldiers said. "Let me see what's in your basket."

Miriam glared at him with hatred in her eyes but he returned her gaze with scorn. Thankfully, he returned the basket after pinching a loaf of flat bread and nibbling it in front of her. "You bake good bread," he said. Then he looked carefully at her wrists, grabbing one of them. She dropped the basket and tried to push him off, but the soldier hung on to her firmly.

"Ah, I see, only one gold bracelet. You must have others under all those clothes. Obviously you are the matriarch of this big family."

"I sold them all," she lied, looking at the soldier straight in the eye.

"Well, well. Ha, if we had a female soldier with us we would make you strip!"

He wrenched off the one bracelet. "We will keep this one as a souvenir," said he, with a supercilious smile.

"Robbers", she hissed under her breath. In reality, prepared for such an emergency, all the women had wrapped their gold bracelets in strips of cotton and sewn them carefully inside their petticoats. Meanwhile, another soldier was making rude gestures at Lily, Lucy's attractive younger sister. Lucy aware of this tried to hold her sister in a wide embrace encompassing her twin boys and Lily at the same time, but the soldier grabbed her shoulder. He slapped her hard in the face and taking advantage of her stunned lack of reaction, he put his hand down the front of her dress and pulled out a cross and chain.

"Ah, I see you are a Christian! Well, you are all the same you dirty Arabs."

One of the men came to her rescue and the soldier cocked his gun to threaten him. Although they were all wearing headscarves, the Muslim women had their heads completely covered, making a distinction between them, which had obviously confused the militants.

"Come on let's go," shouted Amin.

Amin and his sons had already hitched up the donkey to the wagon and everyone scrambled aboard.

"Why can't we go in the car?" one of the twins wailed.

"Why can't the dogs come too?" the other yelled as one of the dogs barked.

"Because we are too many and there is no fuel," answered their father.

Indeed they were really too many for the wagon. Amin did a quick count. There were Miriam, Lucy, Lily, Sawsan, now very obviously pregnant, Mahmoud's new wife Mai, and the twin boys. Then the men were Amin and his three sons, plus Yousif and Issa. Altogether thirteen persons. Miriam was eager to correct him as thirteen was not a good number. "We are fourteen counting the new baby...that is when he arrives."

"He is taking this journey with us," said Sawsan, patting her large protruding tummy and trying to keep back the tears but trembling with fear.

"What will happen to the animals?" the children were voicing everyone else's fears, as they saw the dogs trying to follow them with sad, wounded eyes. Then they were shocked to see one of the dogs shot dead.

"Maybe we will be back soon," said Amin, yet realising as he said it that it would not happen.

Soon a crowd had gathered, men and women, young and old, children and babies. In fact dozens of people, the whole population of the village. Some were on horseback, some in donkey carts, some walking and a few in cars. As they left the village a terrible sight awaited them. The bodies of the Arab guards were lined up in a row on the ground, their gunshot wounds visible and lying in pools of red and purple blood. Some bodies had been left for days and were already bloated by the sun. Cries of disgust and horror went up from the crowd. Some were vomiting, others were fainting and most were sobbing angry tears. The children were confused and distressed as their mothers tried to stop them gazing.

They hurried past and continued downhill and along small dirt paths where the sun had dried up every atom of grass, but where there was some shade from the tall eucalyptus and pine trees. Soon it became apparent that the wagon was too overloaded, so the younger men decided to walk. They had already been on the road for about an hour when they reached the outskirts of Haifa but knew that they had to bypass the city. They could see the sea shimmering in the morning heat and watched the birds flying around in seemingly endless and pointless circles.

Suddenly, Mahfouz, the youngest of Amin's sons put his hands up in the air and started shouting. "Oh God, I forgot,"

"What?" they chorused.

He put his hands over his face and seemed to be really distressed.

"What's the matter?"

"You know I was saving some money to build a house and then get married."

"Well?"

"I hid the cash behind a niche in the stone wall of the house. I found a loose brick and covered it. No-one would be able to find it except me".

"Well, you can't go back for it now," said his father.

"But I must."

They all stopped for a break while the men conferred with each other and Miriam doled out scraps of bread and olives to everyone.

"It is far too dangerous to go back. They will shoot you," said Yousif. He had heard of it happening to others who tried to go back to their homes to retrieve some valuables.

"But I must go back," insisted Mahfouz.

"Please don't," his mother pleaded. "When we get to our destination you will be able to work and start saving again."

"Mama, it is a lot of money, a lot, a lot." He began to tear his hair. "I will wait in the forest then at night time I will creep very carefully to the house. If all the people have gone the soldiers will have gone too."

"Don't be so naïve. They will have guards to stop anyone returning," said Amin.

"Anyway, where is your destination?"

"Lebanon will welcome us."

"It is a long way to Lebanon."

No matter what everyone said or pleaded, Mahfouz was determined to go back. "You go on. I will stay here til nightfall." There was nothing more anyone could do or say.

"I will catch up with you."

"*In-shallah*, God willing," they all said as they hugged him goodbye.

They continued their journey with heavy hearts, wondering if they would ever see him again, Miriam weeping quietly. With so many mouths, the basket became empty quickly. The children were crying with hunger, and Sawsan was cringing with pain in her back, trying to find a position where she could be more comfortable. A lorry passed them piled high with watermelons and two fell off the back. The men picked them up and found them cracked, so they were able to tear them apart and give everyone a small portion. It was enough to temporarily quench their thirst.

After two days the crowds with them began to disperse in different directions, and the problems began to multiply. At one point, the donkey was so tired, he refused to budge another inch. He was getting too old for this anyway. The wheels of the cart were wobbling dangerously, the men were foot sore, the children had cried themselves to sleep and everyone was worrying particularly about Sawsan whose face betrayed her brave front trying not to reveal the pain. Miriam could see the first signs of labour coming on. On top of all of this, every time they tried to stop in an abandoned village, the Israeli soldiers would appear and make them move on. Somehow they did manage to find scraps of food in the villages or fruit from the trees.

Each evening, they tried to find a quiet spot under the trees or in a corner of an abandoned house, which was half destroyed, to sleep, but always their ears were tuned to detect any noise of approaching army vehicles. By night they were bitten by mosquitoes and by day bothered to death by flies attracted to their sweaty bodies. The women had long since taken off their outer dresses, which they used as a covering at night. But they tried to keep cheerful by singing and telling stories.

One day, towards dusk, Sawsan, clutching her stomach, screamed out: "My waters have broken. The baby is coming. I am going to die."

"Where shall we go?" Tha'er, her husband was so alarmed that he looked as if he was in labour too.

"Look, over there in the distance. There are lights," said Lucy.

"It's probably an army camp," someone said.

"No, I can faintly see a cross. There must be a church. Let us go and see."

They took a short cut across the fields until the Monastery came into full view.

"Let me go ahead and see," said Lucy. She jumped down from the cart and ran to the large front door of the building, banging with her fists. The others waited, trying to calm down Sawsan, rubbing her back and pretending not to show fear.

An old man wearing a long brown robe tied in the middle with a white rope came to the door. His middle was as large as Sawsan's tummy. He spotted Lucy's cross around her neck, which she had purposely displayed in front.

"Yes?" he drawled.

"Please help us Father. My 'sister' here is having a baby. Can you give us a room and some water? For God's sake," she pleaded, trying to put one foot over the doorstep.

"Your sister?" The monk eyed the young Muslim woman being held up by two other women, and realised that the middle one was in agony. Then he eyed the men and the two children behind.

"Yes, my sister," repeated Lucy. "Are we not all children of Allah?"

"Wait here. I will have to ask my superior," and he shuffled off down the long corridor.

After what seemed like hours yet must have been a matter of minutes, a younger monk came to the door.

"You are seeking shelter?" he said.

"Please help us," the women chorused.

"Where are you from?"

"We are from a village south of Haifa and we are on our way to Lebanon."

"Come in. You are welcome. I will find a small cell where you can rest. Do you need a doctor?"

"Oh, thank you, thank you. No we do not need a doctor," Then realising the birth was imminent Miriam said: "Could we have a bowl of hot water?"

"The men and children will have to go to our reception room," said the monk. Other monks suddenly appeared and led the men and children in one direction while the women were taken to a tiny cell-like room with just one bed, a table and chair. Tha'er wanted to go with his wife but Miriam reassured him that she could deal with the situation. Reluctantly, he followed the other men, until the monk told him to follow him to fetch the water.

They were just in time. As soon as they had relieved themselves of their bundles, which they had carried on their heads after leaving the wagon, and helped Sawsan on to the bed, it was clear that Sawsan's labour pains were strong and fast.

"I'm going to die," she shouted. Her petite figure seemed to have been overtaken by her enormous belly. They gagged her mouth at first to stop her screaming and lifted up her knees. Miriam, tall and vigorous as ever took control of the situation with Lucy by her side.

"Now when you get a pain, open your mouth and pant like a dog," Miriam ordered.

"Don't push until I tell you."

Meanwhile Lucy laid her hands on Sawsan's stomach and was pushing and pummelling and praying at the same time, while Miriam was peering and feeling up between the legs.

"And you two," addressing Mai and Lily crouching terrified on the floor, "make yourselves useful."

"What can we do?" they squeaked.

"You can soak some clean rags in the hot water," Miriam said.

But the baby was not in a hurry. Two hours passed and they were all panting and sweating, swallowing the drops of salty perspiration that trickled down their faces. Tha'er had brought them water to drink as well as the hot water and now he was pacing up and down the corridor like a convict.

Finally it was time for Sawsan to push, and push she did, like she was going to wrench her heart out. The younger ones held her hands, which she squeezed until they felt she would break their bones. Miriam with her sleeves rolled up high, manoeuvred the baby, who finally entered the world, looking blue and still.

"Come on breathe lad. Cry for God's sake," shouted Miriam giving him a hard slap on his little thin bottom. He suddenly gasped.

"Is it a boy? Is he dead?"

Miriam tied and cut the ugly thick grey cord attached to the baby's belly and held him up slapping him again. He cried but feebly.

Lucy now took charge as Miriam handed her the baby. She rushed out of the room and chased a monk who was walking down the corridor.

"Father quick, bless this baby!"

The young monk hesitated for a second but Lucy held out the baby for him to take. He took it, made the sign of the cross and held him up high. The baby started yelling for all its worth while Tha'er looked on astonished. After all the cleaning up, a woman, presumably the housekeeper, brought them all food and Sawsan was able to rest, happy with her new son, Amin.

THIRTEEN

"…and that scrappy little baby was me."

"You mean your poor mother gave birth to you on the way?" I said.

"Yes, I can't imagine how terrible that must have been for her. And I survived! Incredible."

My father was continuing to recount the story of how his family came to Lebanon in 1948. Now I understood more. My father known to everyone as Abu Farres, had been named Amin, the name of his grandfather.

"Then how come my name is not Tha'er, the name of your father?" I asked.

"It was Granny's wish not to call you Tha'er because of its revolutionary meaning. She said Farres was more appropriate. She hoped that you would one day ride out on horseback with the flag of victory. Not literally of course," he added.

I had many more questions.

"What about your maternal grandparents?"

"My mother always told me they obtained British passports during the Mandate period and went to live in England, but because of all the

119

war and upheavals she never heard what happened to them. I was still very young when my mother died, as you know,"

"So you don't even know what their names were?"

"No, I might be able to find out, though. Anyway, they would not be alive now."

The thought had suddenly struck me...suppose I had relatives in England? If my father could find out their names, maybe Dr Tom could search for any remaining relatives. Maybe their son had gone to England? Maybe...maybe? It was something to think about. I hadn't heard from Dr. Tom since he left Shatila about a year ago, and I wondered if he had received my letters.

"Tell me some more about the early days," I said. We were sitting together on the step looking out at the stars. My father was smoking and I was eating peanuts. It was such a beautiful night and everyone else had gone to bed. Baba yawned. "I've told you bits and pieces many times," he said.

"Yes, but I would like to know the full story," I said.

"Well, my mother told me there were thousands of refugees from the Galilee area of Palestine. The majority of people from Haifa were put on ships but they were only taken as far as Acre. The rest of the journey to Lebanon had to be by car or on foot. I was told that our family came all this way to Shatila, mostly walking or in an old wagon. Some of the people went as far as Syria, but most were too tired to go that far. They decided to make the best of things in Lebanon, so the Red Cross gave them tents. It was a very hard life. They had to queue up for water and food rations from the Red Cross until the United Nations relief agencies took over. There was much disease because of the lack of hygiene and sanitation. Many children died. Everyone had head lice so the medical officers used kerosene on our heads to kill the lice,"

I cringed at the thought. "What about your brother?"

"Yes, he was born just two years after me. You must remember that nobody wanted to settle down because they really thought that they would be returning to Palestine very soon...and we are still waiting after all these years."

"Yes," I sighed.

"Unfortunately, my brother died of gastro-enteritis when he was only six years old.He had been born much stronger than I had, yet I was the one who survived. Two years later my mother became ill and she died too. I think the reason was a complicated pregnancy with her third child."

"Yet Granny survived everyone," I interrupted.

"Yes, she did. It was Granny who really brought me up."

"And what happened to those close friends of Granny's? She often talked about Issa as if he was her son."

My father smiled. "Granny told me that Issa's mother was her best friend. Because they were Christians they probably ended up in Mar Elias camp."

I could see my father was getting tired. He kept yawning, so I decided to give him a break, even though I could have gone on talking all night.

"Goodnight, son," he said. "Maybe one day you will write a book about it all."

"Goodnight, Baba, yes, maybe I will one day."

I must remember to make notes from now. Yes, I thought, I really will write a book about it all one day. Future generations will need to know all about the Palestinians. As I went to bed with my head full of new facts and memories I wondered what I should call my book. Then an idea came to me. I would call it 'Waiting'. For three generations the Palestinians have been waiting for justice and for a return to their homeland. Meanwhile, I was waiting for my exam results, waiting for a new job where I could earn a little money, waiting for a letter from Dr. Tom and Baba was waiting for the baby to arrive. Auntie Lamia, as we called our new mother was due to give birth very soon. Waiting, I pondered, was a very frustrating pastime.

That night, my head was so full of thoughts that I tossed and turned, sleep evading me, but I must have eventually dozed off because at dawn I woke up to hear my father calling me very excitedly. "Farres, Farres, I think the baby is on its way. Go and fetch the midwife." The next few hours were full of frantic activity, but I was kept out of the way. It was a wonderful relief to hear the sudden bawling cry of my new baby brother. I knew that life in our home would never be the same again. For Auntie Lamia, at least, her waiting period was over.

About two weeks later I received my exam results and was overjoyed to learn that I had passed in all subjects and done exceptionally well in English. My family were all very pleased of course and, for once, I got words of praise. Usually it was complaints about my lack of help or bad behaviour. Yet, in the clinic where I still worked, the staff usually praised me for my help and good behaviour! Was I bad or good? I wondered. Perhaps both.

I then heard that there was a job available in the hospital in the neighbour camp. It was very low paid and the work would be a kind of 'dogs body' taking patients to their wards on trolleys and doing errands for the doctors, but it meant that I could still learn a lot and be available for other jobs. I jumped at the chance. I had to learn how to drive a van but that came easy to me. It also meant that I would have a little pocket money. The first thing I would do, I decided, was to write to Dr. Tom and tell him my news. He would be pleased I was sure.

The hospital in Sabra camp, which adjoins Shatila, had been badly damaged during the war and although functioning, it was in a sorry state. Repairs and rebuilding were going on, which meant lots of dust and accumulated rubbish of building materials. The cleaning staff did their best but it was a constant battle to keep the dirt at bay. Many of the original medical team had been killed and in one corner of the hospital there was a memorial stone with the names of the martyrs and some of their photographs. The first thing I did was place a bunch of flowers underneath the memorial stone, praying a prayer for God's mercy.

The present staff were very friendly and positive in their outlook. I was amazed, too at how they made jokes out of seemingly terrible situations. I suppose they did it to keep the morale high.

One morning a few of us were drinking coffee in the duty room next to the emergency entrance. They were teasing me about my unruly hair.

"Next time we're short of a broom we can just hang Farres by his feet and sweep the floor with his hair," someone said. They all laughed as I put my hands through my hair, making it stick up worse than ever.

"Lets call him Farres the *firshay,*" (meaning 'brush').

"No, I'm Farres, the *farashe*! (meaning 'butterfly') said I, waving my arms around.

Suddenly, we heard a loud noise of shouting and wailing as two young lads in their teens were carried in by two men. A crowd of relatives followed them. There was blood all over the place. I helped put them on the examination couches while the doctors shouted orders to the nurses, but I could tell that one of the boys was already dead. I was amazed how quickly the other lad was given an intravenous infusion, oxygen, injections and the wounds in his side and leg treated. He needed further investigations to determine any damage to his kidneys or liver and probably surgery, but their prompt action had irrefutably saved his life. I was awed by their skills, and learned two important lessons for dealing with casualties; first stop the bleeding and secondly replace body fluids. Apparently the boys had borrowed two bicycles and were cycling around the camp when they must have tripped over a wire, which set off the device of an unexploded bomb. One had fallen off his bike and the other boy had landed on top of him. It made me realise that the effects of war continue even after a cease-fire and although I had seen many dead bodies before, I felt quite emotional as I saw the shock on his mother's face and realised that could have been me.

As soon as I came off duty, I decided to visit Mohammed, with the ulterior motive, of course, of chatting with Amal. We often chatted together but nearly always in the company of her brother. I knew it would get her into trouble if we were found together on our own. Amal had the most beautiful eyes, a flawless skin and shiny brown hair, but it was her inner beauty that attracted me to her. I felt she was a soulmate and I knew I was in love. My heart would beat faster just to think about her. The only thing I didn't like was her name!

I knocked timidly on the door and she came to open it.

"*Habibti*", I whispered, then in a clear voice "Is Mohammed at home?"

"Sorry, no", she said, and left me standing.

"Who is it dear?" her mother called.

"Just Mohammed's friend."

"Well, invite him in, dear."

I sat down nervously while Amal fetched me a glass of juice. Her mother came to greet me then disappeared again. I started to tell Amal about the tragic incident in the hospital. She could see that I was personally upset as she murmured sounds of sympathy. I wanted to hold her to me and I felt that she was drawn to me too.

"I love you, you know that, don't you". My voice was barely a whisper. She responded with her eyes.

"But you know that I am hoping to go to England to study medicine, so I cannot make any promises." She nodded.

I wanted to kiss her so badly but instead I took her hand and kissed it. She squeezed my hand, then withdrew.

"We mustn't," she said.

Mohammed and his brother arrived at the same time. They were surprised to see us.

"Where's Mama?" he said.

"Busy in the kitchen."

I blushed and hurriedly bade my goodbyes.

I could hear their mother questioning Mohammed as to why I had disappeared so quickly when I had been waiting for him to arrive. But he saved the day because I doubt whether I could have resisted kissing Amal. It was like an electric current flowing between us.

After that I knew I had to be especially careful, so I tried hard to throw myself into my books and spend any spare time studying. Mohammed sensed my frustration and offered to be the go between if I wanted to send Amal little love notes.

It was hard work at the hospital but I was really enjoying it. After about two months, a new English doctor arrived. He was quite different from Dr. Tom, in fact my first impression was that he was retiring and unsociable but later it turned out that he was shy and that he felt very strange and intimidated by his new culture and surroundings. The language, too, seemed to frighten him. He was much older than Dr. Tom. However, when he discovered who I was, he fished out a letter from his pocket.

"Farres, this is for you from Dr. Tom Jones. My name is James McDonald. I met Tom recently and when I told him I was coming to Shatila, he asked me to bring you this letter."

My face lit up. "Oh, thank you, thank you," I managed to blurt out.

"You speak good English, Farres, would you be willing to give me a few Arabic lessons?"

The ice was broken, but for the time being all I wanted to do was to sit down and devour the letter.

"Of course, I would be glad to," I said.

"See you later, then." He hurried off, his white coat, obviously too small, almost splitting at the seams.

I disappeared into the walk-in linen cupboard and opened my precious letter.

> *Dear Farres,*
>
> *I'm sorry I have kept you waiting so long for an answer, but I am so glad that you are working in the hospital. First of all I have to congratulate you for doing so well in your exams. Well done!*
>
> *Now I think I have some good news. You will have to do two more years at High School here to take some Science subjects in what we call 'A' level. You have to pass these exams before you can go to Medical School. I suggest that you do a six months course first in English, so if you can come early in the New Year you will be ready to go to School in September. When you have your travel document or 'Laissez Passé' ready, I will contact the British Consulate in Beirut to give you a visa. Let me know if you agree to this. I can raise some funds here to help with expenses.*
>
> *In the meantime, keep smiling and God bless you.*
>
> *Tom.*
>
> *P.S. Love to your family.*

I couldn't wait to get home.

FOURTEEN

INTO LEBANON. 1948-1950

Amin, Miriam, and company were very thankful for the few days of rest at the Monastery but on the third day they found themselves on the move again. Providentially there was a truck delivering food to the Monastery. The Arab driver was travelling north to deliver more supplies so he offered to take them some of the way. The donkey was too exhausted to go any further so they left him in the care of the monks. They were glad of the ride even though they had to sit on sacks of rice and beans on the back of the truck. After that they waited for a bus, which took them almost all of the way except for the last half mile which had to be undertaken by foot. Although only a short distance it was a slow drag because of the new mother and baby, because of the small children, and because Yousif developed a fever that made it almost impossible for him to put one foot in front of another.

"Leave me here to die," he moaned.

"Come on Dad, not far to go now," said Issa, as he and the others tried to help him along.

"But I don't want to go to Lebanon. I want to die in Palestine."

Somehow, with the men helping the weak ones and the women carrying their bundles on their heads, they managed to plod slowly forward towards the border. Eventually, the border came into their view but what a sight awaited them. A sea of humanity sitting on the ground, from old people to tiny babies, waiting for their turn to pass through the border. There were border police and Red Cross personnel all trying to keep order in a situation that looked chaotic to put it mildly. Pandemonium broke out as the various bodies tried to distribute bread. Everyone was clamouring for food but some were too weak even to lift up their heads.

As they joined the crowd sitting on the hillock leading to the border, they slumped down exhausted and dejected, not caring even about the stony and thorny undergrowth or the stench of human sweat and other excreta. A loud speaker informed them that they must all register their names and await their turn for transport. This could mean days not hours. The heat of the sun was spiteful and many people had become ill and despairing, willing themselves rather to die than wait for salvation. Others were trying to be patient and cheerful, encouraging the faint-hearted.

Amin and Issa went forward to the refugee office to register the names of their families. Someone nearby heard the name Abu Tha'er.

"Are you Abu Tha'er Kassem?" the young man approached Amin.

"Yes, why?"

"Are you from Al-Tira, near Haifa?"

"Yes, why? Do you have news?"

The young man adjusted his keffiyeh and ran his hand around the back of his neck. He was obviously nervous to tell the news.

"Well?" Amin was also getting agitated.

"I'm afraid to be the bearer of bad news."

"Is it about my son, Mahfouz?"

"Yes. You see I followed him back to the village because I also wanted to retrieve some valuables, but I waited to see what would happen, hiding in the trees. Mahfouz went ahead. He said there were no soldiers. Then I heard some shots and another young boy ran back to me saying that Mahfouz had been shot dead. He was not the only one."

"Oh no," Amin screamed. "Are you sure?"

"Yes…I am so sorry. But there's more," he continued. "The bulldozers were moving in and destroying the houses, even uprooting the fruit trees…"

"Don't tell me any more. I don't want to hear any more," Amin shouted.

Issa put his arm around Amin, trying to comfort him, but Amin pushed him away. He was not only sorrowful. He was very, very angry, shouting abusive words and waving his arms about. Issa had never seen him like this before. Was this the same Amin who seemed always so calm making jokes out of even bad situations?

"They rob me of my land, my farm, my home, my everything and now they kill my son. I knew it. I knew it. We told him not to go back." He was angry with his dead son as much as with the Israelis who had killed him.

Amin was still shouting and punching the air when he returned to the family. It was Issa who broke the news to them all. Miriam took the news remarkably bravely, sobbing quietly but saying that she had known all along that she would never see her son again.

Meanwhile, Yousif was so delirious with fever that he was ranting incoherently. He didn't seem to know where he was or who was his family. Some people nearby gave him some herbal medicine which helped for a short while because he slept, but then suddenly he suffered a stroke. A Red Cross officer passed by and asked if he should send for an ambulance. There were many needing to go to hospital but ambulances were few and far between. By nightfall, Yousif's breathing became more laboured and he died in the early hours of the next morning.

Issa had now lost both parents and the twins had lost their beloved grandfather, but Yousif had had his wish. He died in Palestine. There was no time to mourn and no possibilities of a funeral, so all they could do was say goodbye as the Red Cross came with a stretcher to pick up the body. Issa wept copiously as Miriam, acting as his surrogate mother did her best to comfort him. Lucy, meanwhile, was being a second mother to new little Amin. No longer just friends, they had become a close knit family.

The Authorities gave them permission to cross the border into Lebanon and they soon found themselves looking at a new refugee camp, with people scrambling to put up tents and lining up to register their names for rations. However, other families were waiting for buses to transport them to Beirut, the capital of Lebanon, which was still a considerable distance from the southern border. They were advised to take the bus because they were told that in Beirut there would be more space and more opportunities for work, So that is what they decided to do. Everyone was still thinking this would only be a temporary arrangement anyway, as the war would be over soon, things would settle down and they would all be allowed to return home. Even the news that Amin had heard about the bulldozers moving in to claim his land hadn't really sunk in. No one in the world, however bad the enemy, would destroy his house and farm and never allow the real owners to reclaim it. This was the general thinking all around.

The rickety bus was crammed with people and those without seats sat on the floor, but everyone was so exhausted they slept a good part of the long journey. Finally, at nightfall, they arrived in Beirut and were taken to a suburb of the city, where they spent the night sleeping under the trees of a pine forest.

At dawn, they could hear the roar of the waves and the squealing of seabirds, along with the comforting sounds of the wind in the trees. These were all such familiar sounds for the Haifa family of Issa and Lucy, they almost felt at home, but they woke up shivering, their limbs cramped and aching, conscious that they were really a long way from home. The twins started running around, feeling the damp sea breezes on their faces and excited as they ran up and down the sand dunes. Baby Amin snuggled between his mother's breasts had stopped crying, feeling more secure, as Sawsan his mother, was more relaxed.

The men, all four of them, went in search of food and shelter. They came to a large sandy field where many tents had already been pitched, seemingly in groups of twenty or more. Some women were lining up with old petrol cans to a public water tank. There was an old man supervising the distribution of water who told the newcomers that each family was only allowed one can of water to last all day. The old man directed Amin to the office of the Red Cross, who were temporarily responsible for the refugees. However, it was too early for the workers and they had to wait almost three hours for the office to open. Some of the people in the tents gave them bread, which they took back to their families under the trees.

When the office did open, Amin was the first in line to present himself, giving his name and the names of all his family, but when he mentioned Issa and Lucy, his son Mahmoud intervened. He was a little tired of having to share his life with this Christian family.

"No, Issa and Lucy are not part of our family," he declared to the official.

"Obviously not. They have Christian names," the man said. "How come you are all together then?"

Amin explained that they had been part of their family for some time and since Issa's parents had both died, they felt responsible for them.

"Well," said the official, "I will give you two tents which you can pitch side by side but the authorities might later move the others to another camp."

By the end of the first day they were all settled in their new 'homes'. Besides the tents, they had been given mattresses, blankets, a Primus stove for cooking, some basic foodstuffs, a sack of potatoes, cooking oil, carbolic soap, a tin can for collecting water, and a booklet of rules and regulations. Miriam, the good housekeeper that she had always been was well prepared when they left the village. She and Amin had discussed it many times as to what essentials they should prepare in an emergency, so when they did leave she had bundles ready of sheets, clothes, and cooking utensils. She did not find it difficult to carry huge weights on her head, perfectly balancing them without the aid of her hands to steady the load. From an early age, she had carried sacks of olives and other huge bundles on her head. However, city women were not used to this and Lucy found it very difficult to carry loads without using her hands. Miriam had carried the largest of the burdens when they had to walk, so she was utterly exhausted.

Now the families had to get used to the inconvenience of walking distances to go to the toilet. There were lines of toilet tents in the camp, one for men and the other line facing them for the women. The lack of privacy and embarrassment was humiliating. It was back to primitive basics, but at least they felt safe and they were still convinced that it would only be a temporary arrangement. In fact, even when it seemed returning to Palestine was a distant dream, they would never admit it to each other but continually encouraged one another with a greeting:

'*Inshallah, Allah Kareem*' meaning that God in His generosity would return them to their land.

The other people soon befriended them and were helpful with advice. They told them that on very windy days, even the tent pegs would not hold down the tent, so it was best to secure it with large rocks or big pebbles. They discovered, too, that the sea was much further away then they had first envisaged, as they went to the shore to look for pebbles.

One morning, a group of three young women and their children stood outside the tent, asking for Um Tha'er. Miriam emerged to find her three older daughters and her grandchildren ready to greet her. What a happy and tearful reunion. They were overjoyed to find each other again. They did not have news of the two younger daughters, but they had so much other news to tell each other. Since they had already been in the camp for many months, they were able to warn Miriam of all the problems and pitfalls of camp life. Not only was the wind a problem, when people were constantly chasing their belongings blown away or finding sand in their food, but there were restrictions on water rations and on having to walk a distance to use the latrines, which were necessary for emptying slops. Fines were imposed on people disobeying rules, including the rule of not tipping waste water into the ground. And water was never sufficient for cooking, drinking, washing, etc.

This was Shatila. Inevitably, it did not take long before there were grumbles and quarrels. Amin, without his animals and the constant busy farm life, was depressed. He would sometimes lie in his tent all day.

"For God's sake, get off your backside and look for work," Miriam shouted at him one morning.

"For God's sake, woman, what can I do?" He was angry at being addressed by her so rudely. He had always been in control of her, now the tables were turned.

"Well, go to the labour market with the other men, and see if you can get hired as a labourer on one of those new construction buildings in the city. You are still young enough to work. Why should our sons have to support us all the time?"

"Damn you, woman, I am over fifty and I have worked hard all my life. Just leave me alone will you?"

Miriam looked at her husband with pity. She had always respected him and considered him wise and resourceful. He had always been industrious and creative with a great sense of humorous intelligence. Now he was so laid back and lazy, she couldn't understand it. However, the next morning, without a word, Amin left early with his son Mahmoud to the labour market, which entailed a long walk of almost two miles. There, a whole crowd of men were waiting to be hired as labourers. It was back-breaking work, mixing cement and carrying large stones to be chipped for the building, or bundles of tiles for floors. At the end of one week, they both agreed to do something more interesting, and less strenuous. So, they pooled their meagre wages to buy a barrow. They would sell vegetables and fruit.

This meant that they had to go to the wholesale market at four in the morning to collect potatoes, tomatoes, cabbages, onions, bananas, apples, etc., wheel them in the barrow and sell them in the main street of Shatila. Vegetables were very cheap but they were always needed. Even though most people bargained for prices, Amin had had experience of this before. He was fair and firm. Besides, standing to serve customers was a good way of getting to know all their neighbours, and it turned out to be quite a good little business. At least Miriam noted, Amin's mood was happier and more positive.

Tha'er and Issa managed to get jobs eventually with the UNWRA, a branch of the United Nations which was just starting to set itself up for the welfare of the refugees, taking over from the Red Cross. Issa was lucky enough to get a teacher's job and Tha'er an office job. Education was given top priority in refugee camps and all primary schooling was free, so there was no excuse for any child, boy or girl, not to attend school. When summer was over, the UNWRA set up two big hospital tents to use as classrooms and both children and their parents were very eager to start the new school year. Later on the UNWRA were able to rent some buildings nearby for classrooms. Issa's twin boys, Danny and Sami were now six years old and could hardly wait to go to school.

After education, the second priority was, of course, a mosque. Everyone was asked to contribute a small amount of money to build a mosque, and funds were also collected from abroad. This was very important for Friday prayers and for feasts. Schoolboys were asked to sweep out the mosque on Thursdays, a task they enjoyed doing, not considering it a chore, like sweeping out their tent homes.

Summer was nearly over and the evenings were getting cooler and darker. One evening two men came to the tent asking for Um Tha'er. It was Amin who greeted them but they wouldn't enter the tent. They insisted on speaking to Miriam. One man seemed to be the son of the older man but they were both strangers, probably from another village. They both seemed very agitated and worried.

"Excuse us for disturbing you but are you Um Tha'er?"

"Yes," Miriam said, scanning their worried faces and wondering what on earth would two men want with her.

"Could you come with us to see my wife," the younger man continued. "She is in labour with our first baby and we were told that you are a midwife."

"No I am not registered as a midwife but I have had some experience."

135

Miriam had indeed had some experience, not only in delivering her daughter-in-law but also helping with neighbours. Moreover, she had borne ten children herself and had lots of common sense.

"Never mind that you are not registered. We are sure you will know what to do. Please come with us," they said, their eyes pleading.

"Just a minute, I will ask my husband."

Amin was hesitant to let his wife go out at night with two strange men, but in the end he agreed.

Miriam followed them to the other side of Shatila camp and into their tent. The expectant mother was lying on a thin bare mattress surrounded by a pile of dirty rags. There was a younger girl holding her hand who was a sister to the woman's husband. Miriam knelt down to examine her patient.

"Have you no clean sheets?" she said.

"No, we were unprepared and left in a hurry without anything," they said.

"Then I will give you a sheet. Go back to my tent and ask my husband to give you a clean sheet and my big sewing scissors…" then addressing the young girl: "Boil some water on the Primus quickly."

Miriam took control, as usual, and within a few hours the new mother, who was just a teenager, was delivered safely of a beautiful baby boy. Afterwards, the family were worried that they wouldn't be able to afford the usual fee but Miriam was only too happy to be of help. She had always thought that her family, having lost everything, were really poor, but now she was staring extreme poverty in the face. In the village they would have been considered terribly poor by city standards, but Amin and Miriam had all that they needed. They just lived a simpler lifestyle. This poor girl and her new baby had nothing. There were not even any baby clothes and she had to wrap the little one in rags. Miriam said she would try to find her some things for the baby. They did give her a few vegetables in a paper bag and Miriam felt she had to accept this small contribution, given with much gratitude for her services.

* * * *

Miriam's imaginative cooking and good care took them all safely through the harsh winter. They survived many storms, on one occasion having the tent blown away, and having to put up with the humiliations of walking distances to the toilets, in the mud. Some days it rained incessantly, so everyone was literally living in mud. It got into your hair, your clothes, and the tent. It was impossible to keep clean and families longed for sunny days in order to dry the washing and sweep out the tent.

Amin and Tha'er stood on a small hill overlooking the Camp. The tents were all lined up symmetrically in a regimented order. From a distance you couldn't tell all the disorder and discontent going on inside those tents. It was how they imagined an army camp would look like, yet they had no weapons.

"What have we ever done to deserve all of this," said Amin, his knees shaking and his chin quivering as if he was ready to burst into tears.

"I know how you feel Dad, you have worked so hard to build up your farm, and now it has all gone."

The two of them fell silent, angry, helpless and dejected.

"Good job your Mother is so strong and adaptable," said Amin, as they walked on, not knowing where the future would lead them.

It was a very hard and often depressing life. Many others suffered chest infections and some of the older people died of pneumonia. Tuberculosis was also prevalent. By spring the next year people were scrounging for planks of wood and discarded tin cans which they flattened out to make slightly better dwelling places. Some bought sheets of corregated iron for roofs but the little huts were still very primitive and when the sun shone brightly the metal roofs made it unbearably hot. But, little by little, when everyone realised that returning to Palestine was not going to happen soon, they started to build small houses with whatever materials they could find. Cement, however, was forbidden in those early years. The Lebanese Authorities did not want to see Shatila become a permanent settlement. In fact, although Lebanon had welcomed the refugees at first, it was not long before the Lebanese Government wanted to get rid of their Palestinian refugee brethren.

After two years the Christian families decided to move to another camp where there was a priest to look after their spiritual needs. This camp was called Mar Elias, and somehow Issa and Lucy, their two children, and Lucy's sister drifted apart. By this time Lucy was pregnant again, so that when they moved to a new community with a church, they did not see much of Miriam.

Meanwhile, Miriam had built up a reputation as an excellent midwife and child adviser. Finally, she was earning more money than her husband and everyone in the camp started to call her 'Granny'. It was a nickname that she enjoyed, and she revelled in her new status. All her life she had longed for adventure and independence, now at the age of fifty and in spite of all the privations of refugee life, she felt emancipated.

FIFTEEN

My family was almost as excited as I was. The next few months were going to be busier than ever. I mentally made a note of all the things I needed to do before the new year. There was the question of getting a travel document, and from what people said this was not going to be straightforward. We Palestinians are stateless, we do not live or belong in Palestine and we are not wanted in Lebanon. We are not welcome anywhere! Then I must write notes about all the stories Baba has told me about the beginnings of this camp, about Granny and my great-grandfather Abu-Tha'er, about the Christian family to whom Granny had become so attached, about the terrible massacres in Sabra and Shatila in 1982, about the siege by the Amal militia in 1985 and all that has happened since then. Would I ever have time to sit down and write a book about it all, I wondered. I was also resolved to visit Mar Elias Camp, not far away, and find out if any of Issa's descendants were still alive.

But first, I must write to Dr. Tom, accepting his kind help and asking how I can best prepare myself.

"We are all proud of you, son," my father declared as we were sitting down together for our supper of rice and vegetable stew. Just then the baby started howling in his basket.

"Not you, you rascal. We're talking about your big brother Farres," my father added. We all laughed.

"I'm sure you're proud of him too," I said, as I picked him up thinking what a big generation gap. He had a long way to go before reaching my age of nineteen and goodness knows what the political situation would be by then. As I took baby Ameer in my arms and held him against my shoulder, he calmed down gurgling happily, his big brown eyes laughing as I tickled him. My thoughts turned to the future. Would I be a father, one day? If a son, he would have to be named Amin after my father. So I would become Abu Amin. It was just a fleeting thought before Auntie took the baby from me and hurried away to change him.

Little Ameer would learn as soon as he could talk that he didn't really belong in Lebanon, but that he was from Palestine. If anyone asked him where he was from he would answer a village near Haifa. How many more generations of refugees would it take before there was freedom and justice? My daydreams, as usual, were taking me away from reality. I picked up some dirty dishes from the table and started to put away the bread and olives. My sisters looked at me in amazement.

"Wow, Farres has suddenly become domesticated," they said.

"I guess I need to learn something about household duties and cooking before I go to England," I said.

"I'll teach you to cook."

"Thanks."

Farida is beginning to like me, I thought. Dr. Tom had told me that English men always share the work of the home with the women.

This was a new concept for me. Instead of ordering my sisters around, I should help them. I would have to do some cultural re-thinking.

Next morning I was up at dawn, splashed my face with water and hurried to the hospital. It would be a long day but I was excited and anxious to tell my friends of my plans. I was happy to learn that the boy who had been injured from the bomb was making good progress towards recovery. There was no time for daydreaming. It was just another day of unending fetching and carrying for the nurses and doctors.

"Farres, take this patient to the X-ray."

"Farres, take this specimen to the Lab, please."

"Farres, we need some more sheets; see if there are more in the linen cupboard."

"Farres, we have run out of bandages. Can you please ask for some old sheets that we can make into bandages."

"Farres, we need you to drive the van this afternoon to buy some more stock."

It was good to be busy, but I was very tired when I finally went home, thinking I would just relax. However, when I opened the door, I was surprised to see my father drinking coffee with Abu Mohammed, Amal's father.

"Hello Farres, sit down. We need to talk to you. I think you already know Abu-Mohammed?"

I greeted the visitor and shook hands with him, but was nervous as to what was coming next. My father cleared his throat.

"I think you know Farres why Abu-Mohammed is here? We are concerned that you are putting false hopes in his daughter's head." He produced one of my love letters to Amal. "What is the meaning of this Farres?"

Amal's father glared at me as if I had committed the unpardonable sin. His moustache positively bristled.

"I'm sorry", I stuttered. "It is true that I love Amal, but I have explained to her that I am going away to study. She understands that."

Abu-Mohammed took back the letter from my father's hand and tore it up. "You must stop writing these notes immediately. I can see that you have no intention of marrying her. I have told her if she sees you again or receives a letter, she will be severely punished."

"Forgive me sir. Please don't punish Amal. It is entirely my fault and I promise to stop seeing her or writing notes."

"Good, Farres," said my father, hoping that that would be the end of the episode.

"Sir, I do wish to marry Amal if she can wait for me, but I don't really expect that."

"Certainly not, Farres. We already have a suitable young man in our sights for her," continued Amal's father.

"Then the matter is concluded," said my father in rather stilted terms. Then he beckoned to my sister. "Farida, bring a coffee for your brother, and more cups for us, please."

I fell silent, knowing that the coffee all round would clinch the matter and bring it to a conclusion. I knew it would be difficult to avoid Amal in our close community, and even more difficult to erase her from my heart. We drank from our mini cups silently after which Abu Mohammed got up and shaking our hands said goodbye.

My heart was heavy as I tried to sleep. I was worried for Amal more than myself. What if her father punishes her in spite of all my promises? The next morning, I determined to get up extra early and told Auntie I would go to the street market to buy some more eggs. How could I have known that Amal had told her mother the very same thing? It was impossible to avoid her. We made signs with our eyes to each other, then managed to meet in a corner of a sheltered alleyway where there were no windows to spy on us. There was a pile of rubbish, broken concrete slabs, torn plastic sheets and scraps of rotting food. The smell was terrible though we did not seem to notice it. We were startled by a cat who suddenly sprang from the rubbish, his black fur coloured grey from the dust. Amal and I only had eyes for each other. We kissed passionately and dangerously. Just then we heard children's footsteps, as I realised it was time for the children to go to school. I cupped Amal's face in my hands and kissed her tears. She shook herself free and ran away quickly. I picked up my bag of shopping and hurried home.

"Help yourself to breakfast. Have some of the fresh figs," Auntie said.

"Thanks, but I shall be late for work," I said, grabbing two of the figs and sipping from a glass of hot tea. My mind was in turmoil.

How I managed to get through the day I don't know. I couldn't concentrate and avoided spending conversational times with the staff. I even took some patients' notes to the wrong department, then returned to retrieve them when I realised my mistake.

"What's up Farres? Your mind is not on the job. And where's that usual sunny smile?" the Charge nurse said.

"I'm OK, really. Just too much on my mind."

"I heard you may be leaving us."

"Not yet. I have a lot to do first."

"Well, cheer up and best of luck."

"Thanks," I said. They really were such caring people at the hospital. For the next few weeks, I kept myself busy filling in application forms for my travel document, and also papers which Dr. Tom had sent me. It struck me more than ever when Dr. Tom had talked about passports. I told him for us there was no such thing. Almost everyone else in the world belonged to a country and could travel with a passport, but as Palestinians, we were stateless.

I was also anxious to find out more about Issa and his family. After all it was his father that had given Granny the beads, which she had passed on to me. I had taken them out of my little shoebox so many times and examined them, marvelling at the fact that they had survived at least three generations.

The following Friday when both Baba and I had a day off we decided to go together to look for Issa's family. Mar Elias Camp was only about a mile away so it would not take us long to walk there. I knew hardly anything about them.

"Baba tell me more about this family," I said, putting on my jacket, as the autumn winds and rain had begun.

"Granny did not tell me a lot, only that Issa's wife was called Lucy and she had twin boys, Daniel and Sami. I reckon we shall have to ask someone from the church," he said.

As we approached the main gate I could hear the man in the minaret calling the people to prayer. *Allahu Akbar* was an everyday sound. I turned to my father. "I thought they were only Christians living here," I commented.

"I think a lot of the Christians have left and Muslims from our camps have taken refuge here," he said.

In fact the camp did not look any different than ours. The same squalid looking cement-block houses built higgledy- piggledy, with narrow dirt alleyways in between, dirty water running in the streets, rubbish dumped in piles by the overflowing garbage bins, electric cables swinging dangerously across the alleyways and burnt out cars left to rot at the side of the road. There were crowds of people everywhere. They did not even notice us. I observed only two differences, one was that the girls and women were mostly not wearing headscarves and two, there was a small church built of bricks right in the middle of the square. We approached the church hesitantly. A tall priest, dressed in an ankle length black gown, with a grey beard and long grey hair tied back in a bun, greeted us. "Greetings to you Father. Excuse us we are looking for a family by the name of Issa Farah," my father ventured.

"Ah yes," the priest answered. "I think I can help you. Where are you from?"

"From Shatila Camp, but our forebears came from the same district in Palestine".

"Really, where?"

"From a village just south of Haifa".

"I am from Haifa, too," he said, "But I was too young to remember anything. In fact I was just a baby."

Baba's eyes lit up. "Then we are about the same age. I was born in 1948".

The priest smiled and nodded. "Well, well," he said.

"Is Issa or Abu Danny, as they must call him, still alive? I questioned.

"No, I'm afraid not but his widow is here and her two daughters. Come with me. I will show you where they live." We followed the priest for quite a distance, weaving our way through narrow alleyways until we came to a block of newly-built flats. Climbing the dark cement steps without rails, we eventually reached the daylight to discover a rooftop courtyard adorned with a beautiful array of pot-plants like a miniature garden. It seemed like an oasis of beauty. The priest knocked on the door which was opened by an old woman with curly grey hair and ruddy cheeks. She was almost as wide as she was tall. She beamed a welcome at us even though we were strangers.

"Welcome Father, how are you today?" then to us "Welcome, welcome, come in." My father introduced us. "I am Abu Farres, the grandson of Abu Tha'er." She looked at us trying to understand. Then suddenly, she held out her arms. "Then you must be Amin? Come here let me hug you!"

The emotional hugs and tears were something I shall never forget. "Do you know that I helped to bring you into this world?" she said.

We sat down on a sofa and I looked around at the simply furnished room with its many colourful cushions. There was such a warm, loving atmosphere. Her daughter, who we later learned, was a war widow, was looking after her mother. She brought us some hot tea and invited us to stay for lunch. In spite of my father's polite refusals, they insisted we stay. After tea, the priest got up to go, proclaiming God's blessings on us all.

"So you must remember Granny, Um Tha'er well?" I said, looking into Lucy's kind eyes. "Have I met you before?" There was something faintly familiar.

"Yes, I came to Granny's funeral, but you were just a little boy then."

"Well then I must have met you. It was just before the massacre, but after Baba had left".

"Yes, that's right."

We continued to chat about Granny's life, about the time of the exile in 1948, about the difficult birth that she helped with on the way, resulting in my father's arrival into this world.

"Did Granny Miriam ever tell you that you were born in a monastery and how the monks were so kind?"

"No, I never knew that," my father said.

"I was only 22 years old at the time and already had six year old twins", she continued.

"Yes, I heard. Where are the twins now?" I asked.

"They are both doing well in Canada. It is hard for me to have them so far away, but I have my two daughters here who were born in the refugee camp."

"That is hard. It will be the same for my family when I go to London."

"It is the Palestinian story over and over. We are dispersed all over the world," added my father.

"Please tell us some more memories." I longed to know more about this family.

Lucy smiled, her nostalgic memories taking her into the past.

"There are wonderful happy memories and there are some very sad memories," she said. "Which ones do you want to hear?"

"Both," we said.

"Well, you know we lived in Haifa by the sea, but there came a terrible day in April 1948, when we were all turned out by those Zionist underground forces."

"Was it a proper army?" I interrupted.

"Not at that time but now they are the Israeli army." She continued:

"Well, we didn't know what to do. Some people were going north in trucks, others were leaving by ship and even some were trying to hide, while the Arab armies were retreating. But my husband Issa decided to go south to where Miriam lived. You see Miriam and my mother-in-law, Majida, had always been close friends from their childhood. How we managed to go up those hills with our little car, I shall never know. It was a miracle. Anyway, we were welcomed by Granny, as you call her, and spent a happy three months there, until we all had to leave again in July. There were seven of them and six of us, plus the farm workers. We were a full house but we were so happy together." She started to laugh. "Issa had to learn how to milk the goats and one of them kicked him. Then the twins used to play with the two dogs and had great fun collecting eggs, falling into the pond, riding the donkey and climbing the trees...oh a host of fun things but always getting into trouble as most boys do. There were three of us cooking, Granny,

Sawsan and myself but somehow we all pitched in happily. Then in the evenings, we would all sit together under the vines and tell stories or jokes. Your great-grandfather Amin was a great one for jokes. He was a great help to my father-in-law who was depressed after losing his wife in the fire. You know, my father-in-law died at the border before we crossed over into Lebanon and your father Tha'er was a great comfort to Issa."

"Mother, don't get too tired talking," her daughter intervened.

"Don't worry. These are some of the good memories. I don't want to remember the bad ones."

"Tell us more about the early days in Shatila. Were you the first families to arrive and start the camp?" I asked.

"No, not the very first, but there were not so many in the beginning. We slept the first night in a forest under the trees. Then we were given tents and basic foodstuffs and soap. Ugh! the soap was horrible. We were used to pure olive oil soap but this carbolic soap smelt of toilet disinfectant," she screwed up her face to show disgust.

"What did you eat?"

Lucy laughed. "Shall I tell you what we ate. It was potatoes, potatoes and more potatoes. They were cheap and there was a glut of them. Your Granny used to boil them in their skins and we would eat them with a little salt. When you are hungry you eat anything," she said.

"We know all about that when we were under siege by the Amal militia a few years ago," I said. "Many times we never saw potatoes."

I fished out the green-blue beads from my pocket. "Do you remember these, Um Danny?" I asked.

She took the beads and fingered them on her lap. "Why, these must have originally belonged to my father-in-law, Abu Issa. Did Granny give you these?"

"Yes, she gave them to me before she died and told me to keep them safe."

"That's wonderful. These are really Christian beads. Did you notice the little silver cross?"

"Yes."

"Then you must take care of them. If you ever go back to Palestine, you can leave them there."

"God willing, I will one day go there. Who knows."

Dear, dear Lucy, or Um Danny, as people called her, was as huggable as a teddy bear! We could have stayed talking all day but after a delicious lunch and coffee we reluctantly said goodbye, urging her to visit us in Shatila.

"I may surprise you one day," she said.

"You would be more than welcome," we said.

Sixteen

LONDON 1990

The excitement and nervousness of travelling had invaded my whole body and now I was faced with so many culture shocks. I was in a new world, a new culture, a new environment and a totally different way of life. But I was free! No longer confined to the perimeters of a refugee camp. It was impossible to describe what it felt like to be free.

My farewells at Beirut airport were tearful. My sisters cried the most, though my father was equally emotional without showing it. He kept encouraging me, saying how proud he was to be the father of Doctor Kassem! "Hang on," I said. There are at least seven years ahead of me before I can claim that title…if I make it!"

"You will, you will," he said. "But you will write us letters, won't you?"

"Of course," I assured him.

Now I was in London, having successfully found my way to the departure lounge in Beirut, then in Jordan, where I had to change planes and finally in London. First I found myself in a long queue to go through passport control. I was amazed that instead of being questioned by a typical white Englishman, it was an Indian Sikh wearing a head turban, and sporting a huge moustache, who welcomed me into the country. And he was just as English as anybody. My stereotype thinking was jolted immediately.

"You are a Palestinian?" he said. "But born in Lebanon? No Lebanese passport?"

"No. My family are refugees."

"How long will you be in the UK?"

"I don't know. I have come to study medicine. I have a student visa."

"You are very welcome to this country. I wish you every success."

His wonderful beaming smile was genuine and I really did feel welcome.

After a brief time looking around for directions, I found my luggage and made for the exit. There, true to his word, was my dear friend Dr. Tom.

"You are the second one to welcome me," I said, as we hugged each other.

"Really?"

"Yes, I've already been welcomed by a Sikh."

He laughed. "You will soon learn that London is international and cosmopolitan."

As we left the airport and made for the motorways, I had so many new things to observe. It was January, so most of the trees were bare, but the countryside looked so wonderfully green everywhere. Dr. Tom chatted most of the way, trying to initiate me into the customs and lifestyles of the British. I sensed he was trying to warn me of shocks ahead. He lived in a suburban town south of London and it did not take long before we reached his home.

Tom introduced me to his wife, Liz. She was polite in her welcome, but I was uncertain as to her reaction. Do I really look that strange, I thought? Their small daughter, however, was more forthcoming. She was talkative, like her father. Smiling, she took my hand and led me upstairs to my room.

"What's your name?" I asked.

"Sally."

"Well Sally, how old are you?"

"Just eight. It was my birthday before Christmas."

"Wow, that's wonderful," I said, not sure what date Christmas had been.

"No, it's not good having birthdays around Christmas. I only get one present instead of two!"

"Oh dear!" I said.

"What's your name?" she asked.

"Farres."

"I've never heard of that before." She screwed up her eyes enquiring.

"It means a knight on horseback."

"Oh, just like in the story of Sleeping Beauty. She is woken up from her long sleep by a Prince who is a knight." She looked through her books to find me the story.

"You and I are going to be friends, aren't we," she said, looking out from the bluest eyes I had ever seen.

"We are, indeed," I squeezed her hand.

"You have such a lovely sunburn," she said. "When we went to the seaside on holiday, I got burnt!"

I laughed. "My skin is naturally more brown than yours." I said.

"Will you play with me after dinner? Or read me a story?"

"I would like *you* to read me a story," I said.

"OK, but first Mummy is preparing dinner. Do you like shepherd's pie?"

"I shall enjoy anything your Mummy makes," I said, not knowing what on earth I was letting myself in for. I had vowed to myself long ago that I must accept all that came my way, even if it was different to what I had been used to. Dr. Tom had followed me up the stairs and was showing me the cupboards, the bathroom and all the other amenities. To me they were all luxuries, especially the bathroom. He showed me how to work the shower.

"There is plenty of hot water if you want to take a shower before dinner," he said.

"This will be your home for the first few weeks until you get acclimatized. Then we will look for lodgings nearer your school. Please feel free to ask for anything you might need. On Monday we will take the underground into London and I will show you how to find your way around. Now, come along Sally and leave Farres to unpack."

"I don't know how to thank you," I stammered, as he took his daughter's hand and went downstairs.

The next morning was Sunday and I was woken up by the sound of church bells. I looked out of the window and saw the neat rows of houses with their carefully trimmed hedges, the flower gardens and the church spire overlooking them all. I was up early as usual, but I needn't have bothered. Apparently Sunday is the day for 'lying in'. However, Sally was up too and chattering away as bright as a button. She was dressed in Pooh Bear pyjamas and showed me all her Pooh animals and books. I was fascinated and couldn't help but compare her childhood to the deprived children in the camp. Her collection of books occupied two shelves and she was only eight! I don't remember owning any books except my school lesson books. But I did not say anything and pretended I knew all about her toys. We played together until I heard her mother calling up from the bottom of the stairs. I had been so preoccupied that I had not heard the family get up.

"Breakfast ready, everyone."

"Coming, Mummy." shouted Sally, then to me: "We have bacon and eggs on Sundays. Do you like bacon and eggs?"

Now what should I do, I thought. Bacon was definitely not for Muslims.

Fortunately I didn't have to say anything as Tom had already warned his wife that bacon was not part of my diet.

After breakfast, Tom and I went for a brisk walk. It was cold and frosty but dry. I had already been given a warm jacket. "Can I ask you something personal?" I said.

"Fire away," Tom said.

"Well, when you were in Shatila four years ago, you never mentioned that you had a wife and daughter."

"That's because I wasn't married then. I got married two years ago."

"Then Sally...?" He saw my eyes were a big question mark.

"Sally is not really mine. I have adopted her. You see Liz's first partner walked out on her when she told him she was pregnant."

"You mean they weren't married?"

"No, perhaps you find this hard to understand, but some British couples live together without bothering to get married."

"Oh," I said, "so that's why Sally calls you Tom and not Daddy."

It was the first of many culture shocks. I was in for a lot more before the end of the week.

Monday morning was a scramble for the bathroom, but I had been up for some time, with excited anticipation. Liz and Sally left first for school and work, then Tom took me on the underground, explaining how to buy a ticket, how to change stations, how to look for the colour codes and arrows and how not to converse with strangers. I wanted to greet everyone but although there were some smiles, most were either with their faces in the newspaper, looking blankly into space, or staring at me. I wasn't the only foreigner. There were Indians, Chinese, Arabs, Europeans; people of all ages, sizes and colours. I had to check myself for not appearing to stare at them. The train was so full and we were standing so close together that bodies were pushing against one another and yet everyone was silent. No one seemed at all concerned that bums, bosoms, walking sticks, brief cases and umbrellas were jostling for space. I wanted to laugh but everyone looked so serious that I controlled myself. Tom smiled at me as if he knew what I was thinking. At each station, there was a great push forward as people tried to disentangle themselves.

"Next stop is ours," Tom warned me.

Then when our station arrived, we moved forward, tumbling out of the train as one body.

'Saint Paul's, mind the step', boomed out a voice from nowhere.

We walked to the Technical College where Tom had already registered me for language studies. We were shown to the classroom and Tom took me to the window. "See that big building over there," he pointed out a building in the near distance. "That's the hospital where I work. If you need me at any time, you can come and ask for me. Here, buy yourself a sandwich for lunch and I will be here to pick you up at five. Bye." He was gone and I was on my own. For one moment I panicked, as I continued to stare out of the window. Then one of the other students approached me: "*Btihki Arabi?* Speak Arabic?" I turned round and could have hugged him. Ali was one of several Arab students from Egypt and the Arabian Gulf. We soon became friends. During the lunchtime break Ali introduced me to a snack bar, a place to change money, and the

Post Office. He had been in London for a few months, so was able to fill me in on all the things I wanted to know. I was also glad to be able to send a postcard to my family. The language classes were only three days a week, so I had to find a job to earn some pocket money. Ali took me to a small supermarket where I luckily found a job stacking up shelves. In three days I had already become part of the English scene.

About two weeks later when I was fully confident of finding my way home, I had an experience, which jolted me out of complacency. I had been working late and took my usual train home. I noticed a gang of three young men who got into the carriage with me. They had obviously had too much to drink and were behaving foolishly. They kept watching me but I pretended to be reading my lessons. I could sense that they were not going to be friendly. The train's speed was racing in tune with my heart. They started laughing and using foul language.

"Bloody Arab," one of them said. They all laughed but I took no notice. They continued to verbally abuse me and I was getting angrier and angrier, but determined to stay calm. When there was no reaction from me they started attacking me physically, punching, kicking me and hitting me in the face. The taller one with spiky green hair, obviously the ringleader, was about to kick me when I stood up with my legs apart, deflecting his kick with my left arm then bringing it down across his neck and face. The other two lads stood open-mouthed without a word. He then tried to free his hands to punch me in the stomach but I was quick to pull around behind him, gripping his head in a neck lock. This caught him completely off balance and he could not attack me with his legs or fists. I glanced sideways to see that one of the other lads was fiddling with a penknife, but my opponent screamed at him.

"Put that away, you bloody fool!"

The third lad tried to push me away but I managed to use my leg to trip him. I was so glad that I had taken self-defence lessons in Shatila. For us, kids, Karate had been a kind of sport and lots of fun and camaraderie. In the camp we had no large areas to play soccer and the only other sport was a modified basketball. It was also a way of releasing our anger at the political stalemate and lack of employment opportunities. My training had certainly come in useful in a most unexpected situation.

The train was slowing down and as soon as the next station came into view all three of them ran to the door. No sooner had the train jerked to a stop than they had jumped off. An older man got on the train who was sympathetic and I somehow managed to get home, bruised physically but with my self-esteem intact. Tom met me at the door.

"What on earth...?" Tom exclaimed. I explained what had happened.

"We should call the police," he said.

"No, no, please I don't want to get the police involved," I said.

"It is sad that there are still some people who are racist," he said, as he took me into the kitchen and bathed my black eye.

The next morning a letter arrived from my father and sisters. They had a lot of news to tell me. I learned that my beloved Amal was engaged to be married and suddenly I felt overwhelmed with homesickness. I could not hide my tears.

It was another two days before I had the courage to go back to school. Ali was beginning to worry about me. He gave me some good advice. "Never get into an empty railway carriage," he said.

After a month it was time to move on and I found a cheap youth hostel run by the YMCA not far from the school. However, even this was expensive and I was not eating well. I knew I must find a better job and also apply for asylum so that I would get government help.

Tom said he would ask at the hospital if there were any jobs going. I was prepared to do anything. Eventually, he found me the job of night porter for the casualty department of the hospital. It was similar to the job I had had in Shatila, except that it was at night and the kind of emergencies were very different. They were mostly victims of crime or drunkenness or accidents caused by drink driving. This was not a problem in Shatila, where men congregated in coffee shops and not pubs. Once again I found it a whole new world. I rarely saw Tom as he worked during the day but he turned up one evening to find me busy helping to unload an ambulance. It was so good to see him. He greeted me with a big smile. "How is Mr. Night?" he said. I thought he was referring to the fact that I was working nights. "Sally keeps asking me when is Uncle Night coming home?"

I suddenly twigged. "Oh, you mean Mr. Knight with a K," I said.

"Yes, of course. Sally told me that your name Farres means a knight on horseback!"

"Sally misses me?"

"Yes, too much. She is always asking me when is Uncle Knight coming back".

"I miss her too," I said.

"Well, if you are off duty on Sunday, you must come and have lunch with us."

"Oh, thank you, Tom, I would love that," I said.

He hurried away, waving. "See you Sunday, then."

By the month of May, we were looking forward to the end of exams and a party had been arranged, not just for the language students but also for all the various courses. I was hesitant to go as it was being held in a pub, but Ali encouraged me. "Pubs are part of the British culture," he said. "It does not mean that you have to drink."

"OK, but I don't have anything special to wear."

"You don't need anything special. Just clean and casual."

Of course, at the party, I was practically laughed at when I asked for an orange juice, so Ali bought me a beer and I found that I liked it. It was the first time I had tasted alcohol. Others of course were drinking vodka, whisky and gin. I did not know how they could stand up after several glasses. The food snacks were good but not satisfying. The music was loud and everyone started dancing. I started chatting to a young girl who looked about eighteen but may only have been sixteen. She told me she was doing a secretarial course. She was pretty, with long blond hair and sparkling blue eyes, which were heavily made up with mascara and tinted shadow. She wore a skimpy skirt and a sleeveless top. The weather was spring-like but still chilly in the evenings. The music was noisy but it was a very pleasant atmosphere. We danced together and she was friendly. However, before long she was whispering suggestions in my ear.

"I like you. Would you like to go to bed with me?" she said.

"You mean…?" I stammered.

"Yes, sex, you dummy!"

"Oh, no." I drew away before she could kiss me, so shocked, yet at the same time feeling shivers down my spine and an ache in my thighs. I fetched my coat and walked home as fast as I could. In Shatila I was not allowed to write love letters to my beloved Amal, here the girls were running after me. When I reached my little room, I collapsed on the bed laughing. I suddenly saw the funny side. The name of the pub was 'The Bull and the Maiden' and on the hanging sign there was a picture of a bull chasing a frightened girl. What an upside down world, I thought.

$\mathscr{S}$EVENTEEN

My first year in England was coming to an end and another war in the Middle East was imminent, though this time in Kuwait and Iraq. So many unanswered political questions, so many disastrous political mistakes, so much unnecessary bloodshed. When will the world learn that wars never achieve anything.

I had spent the summer working hard as porter in the hospital and managed to work some overtime hours, which earned me more money. I was also gaining lots of medical knowledge and experience, but from September, I was now enrolled in an A-levels course at a sixth form college in subjects of science. I found Biology comparatively easy but Physics and Chemistry were more difficult to understand. There was so much new vocabulary to learn. The school was in the suburbs of London so I had to change my lodgings too. Together with three other students we rented an old house. It was only a two-bedroom house, which meant we had to share two to a bedroom and also share the kitchen and bathroom. It also meant lots of minor squabbles, but somehow we survived. We were all different nationalities and religions and ironically my first roommate was

Jewish from Ethiopia. I never knew before that there were black Jews. Strangely he was planning to immigrate to Israel and he had never heard about Palestinian refugees. I had long since discovered that many English people didn't know where Palestine was or how Israel had come to birth. I determined to try to educate people about the Palestinian problem and since there was a war in Iraq and everyone was trying to understand the geography and politics of the Middle East, it was a golden opportunity.

Contrary to everyone's predictions, my roommate and I got on very well together. We shared the same jokes and the same cuisine. He liked to cook so we often ate together. He was not religious… and neither am I come to that. The only reason he and his family wanted to live in Israel was for economical benefits. Apparently his family in Ethiopia were very poor. They were promised a much better standard of living in Israel. I tried to explain to him that just because he was a Jew he could attain Israeli citizenship immediately, whereas my family whose forebears had lived in Palestine for generations are not allowed to even enter Israel. He could not understand the injustice of it all. The only thing I didn't like about Solomon was his use of some smelly oil to rub on his skin 'to make it shine' he said.

Meanwhile, I had become thoroughly acclimatised to the English way of living and began to like the food and the habits of the British, though inevitably I still had bouts of homesickness from time to time. My father wrote regularly and I tried to do the same. Tom and his family adopted me for holidays. He had saved my life in Shatila and now I owed everything to him. I was with them for Christmas and New Year and learnt all about this very special feast for the British. I remembered that it was Sally's birthday the day before Christmas so I took her two presents.

"Oh, Uncle Knight, two presents. You remembered!"

"Yes, one for your birthday and one for Christmas," I said.

"I do love you Uncle Knight," she said.

"You are a little sweetheart," I said as I hugged her.

"When I was little," she said, "I thought Santa brought all the presents. Now I know it is Mummy and Tom who buy the gifts. Does Santa come to your land and give children presents?"

"He never came to me when I was a little boy," I said.

She was indignant. "But I was told that he goes all over the world and gives sackfulls of toys to all the children in the world."

"I did get presents on feast days sometimes. It was always new clothes, never books or toys."

"Oh you poor thing!" she exclaimed, then as an afterthought: "Would you like to see our Nativity Play at the school. I am an angel!"

"I would love that," I said. That afternoon Liz, who had warmed to me much more, took me to Sally's school and explained to me the tradition of Nativity Plays. Sure enough, Sally appeared in a long white dress with plastic wings announcing 'good news' to three little kids with runny noses and dressed with Arab keffiyehs on their heads. They were shepherds watching some sheep who were depicted by more little children covered over with sheepskins and crawling on all fours. Then there was the scene of baby Jesus with Mary and Joseph, and our angel in the background. It was hilarious yet serious and magical. The choir of children singing about Bethlehem brought tears to my eyes.

Later, with the Christmas tree lights on and the house all decorated with greenery and bright red flowers, I sat with the family watching television.

"Did you like the play?", piped in Sally.

"I thought it was wonderful," I said, winking at her. "Especially the angel. Did you know that Bethlehem is in my country?"

"No," she said. "I thought you were from Lebanon."

"Yes, but my family came from Palestine."

It was too difficult to explain and I did not want to spoil the programme Liz and Tom were watching on television, so I dropped the subject. Perhaps Tom would explain it to Sally sometime. I was glad that Tom understood.

Christmas over, I returned to my lodgings and found that Solomon had returned to Ethiopia. He used to go around wrapped in blankets, so I suppose the cold was too much for him. I wonder if he and his family will make it to Israel?

One evening, unexpectantly, the phone rang. It was Ali.

"Where have you been? I've been trying to get in touch with you."

"How did you find me?" I said.

"I asked at the school for your number."

"Oh, sorry I've not been in touch. Anyway, it's good to hear you Ali."

"Look Farres, are you free on Saturday?"

"Yes, except I have to work from four o'clock. Why?"

"There is going to be a big anti-war rally and also a peace and justice rally for Palestinians".

"Wow," I said.

"Anyway, meet me in Trafalgar Square by one of the lions, you know where?"

"Sure," I said.

"Right, see you nine o'clock on Saturday then. Bye."

At weekends I usually worked in a local Italian Restaurant. My job was preparing the pizza toppings and washing dishes. I could just imagine my sisters being astonished if they saw me doing kitchen jobs.

Saturday turned out to be mild but grey. There were lots of black, menacing clouds overhead. The underground trains were more crowded than usual, but I was in London way before the time. Ali was early too. A crowd had already gathered, a few sporting Arab head dresses and some carrying large placards proclaiming 'Peace not War', or 'Make Love not War', or 'Justice for Palestine', or various other statements.

Many organisations were represented and the people were a mixture of Christians, Muslims and Jews. It was exciting to be marching alongside like minded people, and it was good to be with Ali again. The scene soon became chaotic. Hundreds of policemen were employed to control the crowds and to cut off the roads from traffic much to the annoyment of motorists who were honking their horns like mad. There were also reporters everywhere ducking in and out of the crowd with cameras and microphones.

"Just a word of warning, Farres," Ali said. "Some people will be shouting slogans against the British and American Governments, against Israel too. It is best to keep a low profile as much as you feel like shouting. The police will be watching out for trouble makers."

"Oh, don't worry Ali, I will keep quiet!"

"Wait and see, there is bound to be some noise and violence. People are easily worked up into a frenzy when they are passionate about a cause. I know you are passionate about the cause of Palestine."

"Yes, true, but I'm not going to risk arrest or deportation."

"Good man," said Ali.

As it happened, though, I did find myself getting worked up and started shouting a chorus with other Palestinians: 'P...L...O, Israel NO'. We were chanting it slowly and deliberately. It was a chorus I had learned as a child but I discovered that it was one thing to sing it in Shatila and a totally different thing to sing it in London. Meanwhile I had somehow missed Ali in the crowd and was caught up being pushed along the streets by the melee. Some policemen approached us and I quickly remembered what Ali had said. Before I could move forward, a burly policeman towered over me and grabbed me by my arm. I thought that I was tall but he was a giant in comparison. His kindly face broke into a huge smile. "Sonny," he said. "I'm sure you don't want me to arrest you."

I was indignant, my face burning. "I thought this was a country of free speech!" I said.

"Just giving you a warning. I'm not taking your name this time," he said, letting go of my arm.

"Thank you," I said, mingling once again with the throng. Within seconds, the heavens opened and the rain poured down in torrents. Some were prepared with umbrellas and continued their walk, but I decided to quit and ran for shelter. I rolled up my coat collar against the wind and stood in the entrance of a small restaurant to shelter from the rain. The smell of freshly baked doughnuts and the strong aroma of coffee were too much. I fumbled in my pocket to see if I had enough money to venture inside. Just then a voice caught me off guard. I looked up into the face of a young woman with light brown hair and mahogany eyes. She was dressed immaculately in a prim navy suit and a white blouse covered by a black overcoat.

"Are you Palestinian?" she said.

"Y..es," I stammered.

"Excuse me for intruding," she offered to shake my hand. "My name is Kate and I am a reporter for the *London Evening Standard*," she continued. "Would you mind if I interviewed you?"

"OK, but I'm not sure if I want my name in the paper," I said, wondering where that would lead.

She ignored my hesitancy and said: "Come on, let's go inside. I'll buy you a coffee."

We sat at a small table in the window with the rain lashing against the panes. She apologised again. "I don't mean to be rude but what is your name?" she said.

"Farres."

"Farres, I am very pleased to meet you. Have you been in London long? Where do you come from?" she produced a small notebook and ordered coffee and doughnuts for the two of us. How could she have read my thoughts?

I answered all her questions as well as I could. I told her about my life in Shatila Camp, that my ancestors came from Northern Palestine, about my family, about the 1982 massacre, about how Dr. Tom had saved my life and enabled me to come to England to study medicine. My coffee was almost cold by the time I'd finished.

She was attractive but not pretty in the usual ideal of feminine prettiness but her voice was soft and deep unlike any other female voice. Usually I find most women have a high-pitched, sometimes grating voice. She was writing a lot down in her notebook, which slightly unnerved me.

Suddenly, someone barged in on us slapping me on the back. It was Ali.

"Hi, Farres. I saw you through the window. You're a dark horse! A fast one too!"

I blushed. He continued to tease me in Arabic until he realised that she was smiling and seemed to understand some of the words. I interrupted his insinuating banter.

"This is Kate. She is a reporter for a London newspaper." I said, matter of factly, pulling up another chair for Ali.

"Oh, pleased to meet you Kate."

"Where are you from?" she said.

"I'm from Egypt. Farres and I were in language school together studying English."

I looked at my watch. It had already gone half past two. Where had the time gone?

"Oh my. I have to dash. I am supposed to start work at four."

"Hang on, before you go, here is my card. Please tell me your telephone number," Kate said.

I quickly recited my number as I put on my coat and hurried out. "Sorry to dash. Thanks for the coffee. Bye."

Ali followed me out.

"See you," he said, waving, as he ran for the bus while I looked for the nearest underground.

I bought the evening paper for several nights, but there was only a short paragraph about the demonstration and march. There was certainly no mention of my name or any other Palestinian. I began to wonder if Kate was a genuine reporter. I dug deep in my pocket and found her card, which read:

'Kate Zuayter, Junior Correspondent, London Evening Standard'. I could not believe my eyes. Her first name was English Christian, the second one Muslim Palestinian.

Which was she?

EIGHTEEN

The image of Kate continued to haunt me somehow. I wished I had asked her something about herself instead of me answering all her questions. By the way she had smiled when Ali was teasing me I realised that she must understand some words of Arabic. The only phone number on her card was that of the newspaper, so I had no way to contact her again. Anyway, I kept telling myself, she was not my kind of woman. Probably too well-educated, too sophisticated, too classy, too English, too professional…too many negatives altogether. She was probably a lot older than myself as well. Beside, the more I thought about it, the more I would tell myself that I was very foolish to even think about her. I shall never see her again anyway.

My studies must come first. Final exams were coming up in a few months' time and I was not ready. I spent all my extra time, when not in class, in the library, and all my evenings with my head in my books.

Ali, bless his soul, kept in contact by phone but rarely was I free to go out with him anywhere. I told him I had too much study to do and was not free to go to any pub or place of entertainment.

"Wait for the summer," I said. "If I pass my A-level exams, we will really celebrate." Meanwhile, I was devouring the news on the communal television about the Iraqis being driven out of Kuwait and Saddam being threatened. Most of all, I was horrified to learn of all the road blocks and continued brutal occupation of the Palestinian territories in spite of so-called international peace talks. The media did not give the true picture, I knew, so some evenings I went to an Arab restaurant not far away where they could tell me more news from folk who were actually in Palestine. There I often treated myself to a falafel sandwich, which was a welcome smell from home. I remembered the little street stalls in Shatila where an old man and his son made their living from deep-frying falafel and selling sandwiches in gorgeous fresh flat loaves, stuffed with salad, sesame sauce and pickles.

One evening, out of the blue, already in my pyjamas, having had a shower, I ran down the stairs to pick up the telephone, which had been ringing for ages. The other two housemates were out and I hardly saw them from one day to the next.

"Hello," I said, expecting Ali's voice.

It was that lovely soft, deep voice again. I was excited in spite of myself.

"It's Kate," she said. "Do you remember me?"

"Of course," I answered. (How could I ever forget that voice?)

"I'm sorry not to have been in touch," she said. "I just wanted to ask you what you thought of the situation in Palestine. Do you think they are serious about peace?"

"Are you going to report my statements in your newspaper?" I said.

She laughed. "No, just felt like asking your opinion, that's all."

"Well, to tell you the truth, I would like to believe in a peaceful solution, but I am still a bit sceptical," I said.

170

"Yes, I thought so. We must meet again for a coffee sometime. I like your frankness," she said.

"I would love that."

My mind was in a whirl. Should I ask her about her background? I must not sound too enthusiastic about meeting her.

"Just to straighten out some of the political issues, you understand…from your point of view."

"Yes, of course."

"When and where?"

"Where do you suggest?"

"I tell you what," she said. "What about that coffee shop at Marble Arch where we first met. Two weeks from Saturday about eleven in the morning?"

"Sure," I said. "That would be great."

"I look forward to seeing you there then."

"My treat, this time," I said.

"Alright, if you insist. Bye."

She sounded too polite and much too professional. I must control my excitement. She is not interested in me, only in my political views. I determined to put her out of my mind, yet at the same time looking in my diary to count the days. It was ludicrous.

A few days later, another call came from Tom, inviting me to a special event at Sally's school. I looked in my diary and found it was the same Saturday that I was meeting Kate.

"What time is the school concert?" I asked.

"Six in the evening," he said. "Can you ask for a free evening?"

"I guess so. It's just that I am going up to London that Saturday morning and meeting a journalist who wants to quiz me about the Middle East situation and whether I think peace in Palestine is possible."

"Oh, what's his name?"

"It's a 'she' and her name is Kate Zuayter."

"Sounds interesting. Why not bring her with you to the concert? I would like to meet her."

"Oh, I don't know if she is free."

"Anyway, Sally is missing you and says you must come to her concert. She is part of the choir."

"I miss Sally too. She is my little sweetheart!"

Tom laughed. "See you soon then. Bye."

I hung up. Two dates with the two women in my life on the same day!

The next few days I studied harder than usual. Will I ever get my brain to understand things like empirical and molecular formulae or extracting aluminium and titanium or concerning electron configurations in atoms and ions or even the shape of molecules? Will I ever get my tongue round terms such as homogeneous or heterogeneous catalysts or that a substance called epoxythene is made from ethane and oxygen? I wondered sometimes if all this knowledge was necessary for my future medical studies and I knew I needed help. Biology and the exciting new field of genetics I found really interesting. I decided to get in touch with one of the English students who was very bright and see if he could spend some time with me to clarify many of these subjects.

Peter lived nearby and was very willing to help. Sometimes I would go to his house, other times he came to me, but we got on well and I found him most helpful. He was the serious studious type, a typical nerd, as they call them, and was often bullied at school for being a bookworm. I liked him and as we got to know each other better I found that he had a difficult home life, his father abroad most of the time and his mother working. Since he was an only child he was rather lonely. Books, for him, had become a kind of escape, a door to hide behind, whereas for me, they were a window into a new world.

* * * *

It was a glorious spring day with the cherry trees in blossom and hope in the air. I felt as happy as a little schoolboy and couldn't help but whistle some Arabic tunes on the underground. Everyone stared at me, except for one old lady who smiled and said she wished everyone was as happy.

"Lovely spring day," I said to her as I fished out a couple of daffodils from my bunch and handed them to her.

"Oh, thank you," she said, her face lighting up as if I had given her gold.

I had bought a bunch of daffodils to give to Kate. Ali told me it was a nice thing to do, to win a girl's heart. The only problem was that I wasn't sure whether I wanted Kate's heart. After all I didn't really know her. This time I had dressed more carefully and had a haircut. I remembered when we met the first time I was soaking wet by the sudden rain storm, and my hair, which is usually unmanageable anyway was a greater mess than usual.

Kate was on time. I imagined her life to be tidy and punctual in the extreme. She was all smiles when I handed her the flowers, and thanked me in Arabic

"*Shukron, Shukron,*" she said, shaking my hand.

"So you understand Arabic?" I ventured.

"No, only a few words. My grandparents speak Arabic," she said.

We sat down at a table in a corner and she took off her jacket to reveal a very pretty pale blue blouse, which matched the colour of her eyeshadow. This accentuated her honey-mahogany eyes. I watched her every movement.

She looked me up and down. "Farres", she said, "you look different?"

I put my hands through my hair, a habit I had had since childhood, but since my hair was shorter it didn't make the usual impact. She laughed out loud.

I was embarrassed but realised she was not laughing at me, she was just remembering why I looked different. "Of course," she said. "It's your hair. I liked it better the last time"!

"Oh dear," I said. "I thought I had better straighten myself up a bit, since I am meeting a lady." We both laughed and the ice was well and truly broken. As we drank our coffee and ate our delicious jam doughnuts we talked and talked, or rather she asked the questions and I did all the talking. I told her of my hopes for the future, of one day being a doctor and maybe, just maybe, going back to help Palestinian refugees. I told her that I was a little sceptical of the peace talks but trying to be hopeful that one day there would be an independent sovereign State of Palestine, but that it all seemed like a dream in the clouds.

"My people have been waiting for a long time to go back to Palestine," I said. "But they have never given up hope."

"I admire them," she said. "And I admire your aspirations."

"Thank you," I said, as I reached across the table and touched her hand. She took my hand and slightly squeezed it. Then, probably feeling embarrassed, she got up and was about to put on her jacket.

"Oh, please don't go yet. I want to hear about your life. I have been doing all the talking about myself. Is your name Palestinian?" I asked.

She sat down again and looked at her watch. "OK then, I have a little time."

She told me that her grandfather had come to London as a young man, with his parents from Palestine. She thought maybe they were from Jerusalem, she wasn't sure. Her father was born in London and her mother was Irish so she was a mixture of Palestinian-British, a mixture of Muslim-Christian.

"I don't quite know where I fit", she said. "But I am studying for a degree in journalism and hope to go to Palestine and Israel to work there for a time. Perhaps you could help me learn Arabic", she said as an afterthought.

"I would be very happy to do that," I said. "Once I've got through my exams." I told her about Sally's school concert and asked if she would like to join us but she said she had work to do. She was just about to leave when she suddenly halted.

"I've just had a thought," she said. "My uncle belongs to a businessman's club, a kind of luncheon club. They are always looking for interesting speakers. Would you be willing to speak at one of his club meetings…about Shatila and your experiences there?"

"I would be honoured, but I'm not sure my English is good enough," I said.

"Oh, they won't mind if you make mistakes."

"When?"

"I will let you know, probably in several months time. Anyway, after your exams."

"Thank you," I said, not sure as to how to say goodbye.

"Well, goodbye Farres, until we meet again." She patted me on the shoulder.

I hesitated for a second then gave her a quick peck on the cheek, which surprised her but seemed to please her. She hurried away with her bunch of daffodils, while my feet took me to the underground but my head was in the sky.

That evening, after the concert, Tom invited me back for a meal. Sally was as exuberant as ever. She persuaded me to play 'Snakes and Ladders' with her after supper. It was the only game in Sally's collection that I knew from my childhood. In Shatila, the snakes were always the 'enemy' and the ladders the victorious conquerors, the Arabs. I made the appropriate hissing sounds when Sally's counter landed on the head of a snake and she had to go backwards, then whoops of victory when my counter landed on the foot of a ladder. Likewise she made the same sounds for me and she ended up winning. She giggled incessantly as we played on the floor in front of the sitting room fire.

"Oh, Uncle Knight, you are funny," she said, slapping me on my leg.

"You're my best girlfriend in the world!" I said.

Tom came into the room handing me a steaming mug of tea.

"She's your best girlfriend? How many others are there?"

"None yet!" I laughed.

"What about this Kate? She sounds interesting."

"No, we're just friends," I said trying to sound convincing, though my face probably betrayed me. Tom knew me too well.

"Well," he said, sounding very serious. "Don't get too involved. You have a lot of years of study to do before thinking of making a commitment to a girl. Farres, you know what? I think you would make a very good children's doctor."

"A paediatrician?" I hardly knew how to pronounce the word. "Maybe," I said.

Tom handed me some forms to fill in regarding Medical School. He had already put my name forward and even had the promise of funds for a scholarship. I was a very lucky young man!

NINETEEN

I scanned the huge notice-board in the corridor of the Medical School to find my name. Had I passed the first lot of exams in Physiology and Pharmacology? I found my name half way down the list. K is in the middle of the alphabet: Farres Kassem. Yes, I had passed. Glory Be! One of the many hurdles over, but still a long way to go. "Come on Knighty, let's go and celebrate at the pub," said my new friend. Hardly anyone called me Farres. My name had deteriorated into Knight or Kassy or more often 'Naughty Knighty', with all sorts of other appendages. The main thing was that I had been accepted as one of the students. I had had to compromise some of my religious customs, though not my faith as a Muslim. I still believed in God and in His sovereign will, though I did not participate in the prayer rituals.

The Medical School was situated in a city south of London. It was a beautiful old red brick building, surrounded by large acres of ground. There were lots of trees and flower gardens, also a football field. The Halls of Residence, where I had my own bedroom was a short walk from the school and not far from St. Mary's General Hospital. My bedroom window overlooked a large chestnut tree, which I watched

177

often to note the changing of the seasons. Somehow it inspired me to know that the tree had seen many generations of medical students and doctors. It was probably much older than any person still alive.

Student life was not at all like I had imagined. I had always thought it would be a very serious place where the student would-be doctors would pursue their chosen career with gravity and in earnest. How wrong I was. There was a minority of medical students with a religious or idealistic approach that they were going to alleviate the sufferings of mankind through their skills. These students tended to lock themselves away in their rooms in order not to be tempted by all the social clubs and drinking parties. On the other end of the spectrum there were students who didn't really want to be doctors but one or both of their parents were in the profession and so had been pressurised into it and because they didn't know what else to do. I found that very bizarre. Then there were some, I discovered, whose parents were able to finance everything and who entered university with the sole purpose of living a drunken, promiscuous life. Some of these were brainy so could somehow scrape through exams, but others failed every time and soon got bored of their free sex, drink and drugs.

I hoped I did not fit into any of these categories. My new found friend…another Peter… and I, were there because we really wanted to study medicine, yet at the same time enjoyed a social life without excesses. Both of us liked a glass of beer to help us relax and both of us flirted with pretty girls, chatting and teasing, but we decided that we would not get involved in any relationship even a one-night stand as they called it. Peter and I were seen so often together that some students thought we were gay, just another British 'fashion' that I found strange and rather shocking, especially the openness of it. I think I had now reached the point where I couldn't be shocked by anything anymore.

So how I came to be 'Naughty Knighty' I really don't know. I teased a lot which people seemed to like. The professors were a motley bunch but most of them were really nice especially the female ones. Although I wasn't up to date on general knowledge such as British politics, historical heroes, famous film stars, or pop idols, I had a lot more knowledge about Middle Eastern politics and had experienced life in the raw in the refugee camp.

One evening we were told that we were going to go to the dissecting room for our anatomy class the next day. A group of us were sitting in the lounge drinking tea after watching a murder mystery play on the television. It was about a young girl who had gone out jogging in the park a few days before her planned wedding. She had been viciously attacked, raped, and murdered, then her beautiful body dismembered. The plot was all about this weird detective trying to work out the identity of the criminal. Of course the story had a twist in the tail as always in these '*whodunit*' dramas. There were various grunts and groans from the students as all was revealed and we ended up giggling. Someone turned off the television and put on a record of loud music.

"For God's sake man, turn that down," said one of the girls, putting her hand to her mouth to stifle a yawn.

"Well we had all better turn in. We shall all be cutting up bodies tomorrow." The tall young man laughed, opening his shirt and slapping his hairy chest.

"Are you afraid?" said one of the other students, turning to me and obviously quivering in his shoes.

"What about?" I said.

"About seeing dead bodies, about dissecting them?"

"Have you never seen a dead body?" I asked.

"No, when my grandmother died, I went to the funeral but I never viewed her body."

"Oh, then, of course, the first time it might be difficult for you, but don't worry, you will get used to it."

"Why? Have you seen a dead body?"

"Unfortunately lots. My own sister was raped and murdered and I worked as a porter in a hospital where I saw lots of blood, bullet wounds and dead bodies." I volunteered.

His eyes opened wide and his mouth dropped.

"Really, Wow. Come and listen to Farres, guys."

The others changed their minds about going to bed. They all gathered round to hear my story. I related to them about the massacre. How I went to the site with my mother and saw the terrible sight of all those bloated corpses, heaped one on top of another, how the sun had made their naked bodies swell so that they were blue and grey, the skin peeling off, some of them with heads severed, children with limbs missing, girls with amputated breasts, how I thought I recognised my sister but did not tell my mother. How the Red Cross workers had brought in bulldozers to scoop up the bodies and tip them all into a mass grave and how the stench of death was so overpowering we felt sick for days afterwards.

I paused to watch their faces. You could have heard a pin drop.

"You're a good storyteller, Kassem. I don't believe a word." The tall fellow with the hairy chest got up waving his hand as if to dismiss the fiction, but noticing the faces of the others, who had gone pale.

"It's true," said my friend Peter, "I know Farres would never make all this up".

"We never heard about this," said one of the girls.

"That's because you were just kids. I was barely twelve at the time."

Overnight I gained celebrity status as if I had acted in some horror movie. This was far worse than the gruesome details of the film we had just watched. Everyone wanted details of my experiences, and when I told them about the episode of my finding the dead baby's hand they were appalled but fascinated. In fact, I think some of them still thought I was making it all up. It took a lot to convince them I was telling the truth.

"I was shot, too, and nearly died," I said, but by this time I had already said too much. They couldn't take any more. At this point too, I had become emotional with so many bad memories. I went to bed with a mist over my eyes and could not sleep for a long time but then I got out Granny's worry beads, no longer in a shoe box but in a small plastic bag. Fingering these and praying seemed to bring me comfort.

Next morning, we were taken to a basement room where there were several cadavers laid out perfectly naked on cold marble slabs. The students tried to hide their emotions but I could see that some were really scared and embarrassed. One poor girl fainted and had to be carried out. The smell of paraldehyde was quite strong and not very pleasant. We all donned white smocks which were mostly either too big or too small, but it made us look very professional. The professor, also wearing a white coat, entered the room. He had receding grey hair, a pointed grey beard and thick-rimmed glasses. He was accompanied by a much younger man who was clean shaven and without specs.

"Good morning everyone. My name is Dr. Ed Hetherington and my assistant here is Dr. Mike Brown. I am going to split you up into several groups and each group will work on one of these cadavers for the term. Each of you will have a turn in dissecting an organ as we study it. You will notice the strong smell of paraldehyde. You will soon get used to this."

We were then divided up into groups of six or seven. Some of us were studying coloured diagrams and plastic models of anatomical parts, while others were shown how to dissect, to get hands on experience. The body in front of us was that of a middle-aged man but his face was covered with a cloth so we could not make out his features. That made it somehow easier as if it wasn't really a person. The professor opened up the chest cavity, tearing back the layers of skin and muscle to expose the lungs and heart. He then explained to us how the circulatory system worked, and how the heart was vital in pumping oxygenated blood around the body. I wondered why the myths about the heart being the seat of emotions when really it was the brain, an organ so complex that even the most learned professors did not fully understand. I found it all very fascinating and even exciting. The smell of chemicals was certainly more agreeable than the smell of blood and rotting flesh.

The rest of the week was filled up with lectures. Besides Anatomy and Physiology, we had to learn Biochemistry to do with the magic codes of DNA, and Pathology, about blood and bacteria, as well as so many other related subjects. I was laden down with books and spent much time either in the library or in the computer room. This was a new technology that I had had to learn before coming to medical school. I had figured that weekends would be free for social events. Wrong again! We spent each weekday evening having fun, either at the Medbar for cocktails…that is if you wanted lots of cheap alcohol…or, in my case, going to room parties with rowdy games or, in playing sports, such as indoor badminton. Then at weekends, we would spend all our time studying and writing up course work.

There were various leisure clubs or societies to join. Some had names more peculiar than the individuals who ran them. Goodness knows what the aims were but they did a lot of badgering to get people to participate. Then there were the secret clubs, where you had to find out the current password to even get acquainted. I had my secret suspicions that these were either cults or drug dens. Peter and I went for the soccer and amateur dramatics at first. I knew nothing about football or drama. I could kick a ball and I could act the fool. Later, I discovered that football had strict rules of play and that drama tended to be an excuse for girlfriends and sexual conquests. So, in the end we opted for safer and more interesting pursuits such as running, badminton and writing poetry. There were also Muslim societies, mainly for Arab students from the Gulf countries who were from rich families. Apart from the Arabic language, I found I had nothing in common with these guys.

For the first year we ate in the university dining halls. The food was good and sensible, but for the students who lived off campus there were all sorts of dreadful stories. Most of them had no idea how to cook the simplest menus and more often than not bought awful junk food resulting in all sorts of stomach upsets. When I did live off campus I certainly knew quite a bit about culinary skills, having learnt from my sisters, my old flatmate Solomon and English food from Tom's wife.

I often craved sweets like the Palestinian sweet pastries called *baklava* but this was difficult to find except in London. Next best thing was sticky doughnuts but these inevitably brought memories of the little coffee bar at Marble Arch.

Kate was abroad. She had gone to Palestine with a photographer and a team of reporters to make some kind of documentary about the Palestine/Israel situation. I was envious to the point of being really jealous. We had become quite friendly but that was all. She always gave me the impression that she did not want any emotional attachment. Perhaps she already had a boyfriend, although she never mentioned it. Her face and her voice were never far from my thoughts however. In fact it was impossible to forget her. She had sent me picture postcards which I had stuck to the wall of my bedroom; scenes of The Old City of Jerusalem, the Dome of the Rock, the Mount of Olives, as well as scenes from Galilee. The greetings were brief and non-committal like 'Wish you could see all these wonderful sights' or 'Am working hard, but enjoying myself'. I wrote back to say how much I missed her.

The last time we saw each other was over three months ago during the break for the New Year. She had taken me to a women's meeting where there was a large group of activists, who were campaigning for justice and human rights for political prisoners. I spoke to them about the need for justice for Palestinian refugees. They were very sympathetic and took up a collection for me, which not only helped me pay for books but also enabled me to send some money to my father.

Kate had introduced me to her Uncle who arranged for me to speak at various clubs, even church groups and this had given me more confidence for public speaking. This had also kept me busy during last summer's vacation before I entered Medical School.

The chestnut tree was dressed in its full glorious clothing of leaves and flowers. The days were getting warmer, reminding us that summer was not far away. That also meant exams and the end of the first year. Apparently it was an unspoken rule that the six weeks before exams had to be devoted to total study, swat, swat and swat. For a time, no more socials, no more wild parties. I hardly knew where to start. So many subjects, so much material to cover. I decided to set myself a timetable.

One evening, sitting in the library, Peter ran up to me.

"Knighty there's a phone call for you... a girl. Would it be Kate?"

My hands were trembling with excitement, as I took the phone.

"Hi Farres, how are you? I'm back."

"Kate, wonderful, when did you get back?"

"I missed you Farres."

"Did you really? I missed you terribly. When can I see you?"

"I know you are busy studying so better wait til after the exams?"

"Oh no. I can't wait that long. Can you come here on Saturday?"

"OK. I'll try to be at the entrance of your Hall of Residence Saturday afternoon."

"Great, I can't wait."

"What about your study?"

"I'll rearrange my schedule, don't worry. I need a break."

We chatted for a while longer, then we hung up. I noticed Peter in the background.

"You were listening, weren't you?"

"Sorry old chap. I am only concerned for you. Sounds like you are serious about this Kate."

"No we're just friends," I said.

"Come on, Farres. I'm beginning to know you better than that. You can't fool me."

"Well, you're one to talk. What about Sarah? I see her sneaking into your room sometimes. What about our promise not to get involved with relationships?" said I. Peter had no answer to that. It seems we were both breaking our promises and it was the beginning of a slight rift between us.

I could hardly wait for Saturday. I planned in my mind what I would say to her, how I would behave, but I knew that this meeting would be important, one way or another. Would she try to keep our friendship as platonic? Was I in love with her, or was I just imagining, dreaming?

Saturday turned out to be cloudy and showery. I had my lunch, then sat in the lobby of the building. Was she coming by train or bus? I had not discussed transport with her. In the end she arrived in style by car! She looked stunning in a blue trouser suit, with a low V-cut white sweater underneath, her brown hair and eyes shining as always. We greeted each other formally.

"Kate, you look great as always," I said, putting my hands through my hair with nervous excitement.

"You look great too, Farres."

"Come on let's go to my room."

"Is that allowed? Why don't we just sit here or take a walk?"

"It's raining. Haven't you noticed?"

"Yes, the first time we met it was pouring with rain, remember?" She laughed.

I led her upstairs to the second floor as I chatted. "I've put your postcards all around my room and now you must tell me all about Palestine."

"Cup of tea?" I asked.

"Yes, please."

She sat in my chair while I went to the corridor kitchen to put the kettle on. We drank tea while I sat on the bed and let her relate to me all about the experiences of working in Jerusalem and the West Bank. I had kept up to date with political developments from television news and the internet, but was hungry for details. I could hardly believe that she had actually been there. She had so much to tell me.

"Farres, I want to hear all about you now. How is life here? How are studies going?"

"It is hard work but I am enjoying it," I said. I told her that I was surprised that the majority of students used more of their time to drink and have parties, leaving all the cramming to the last few weeks. She nodded as if to tell me that this was normal behaviour in all colleges.

We seemed to come to a stop. What more could we say to each other. Why was she keeping her distance?

She got up as if to go. "Come and see my car," she said.

"It's your own car or the company's?"

"My own, I've bought a car, second hand of course, but it serves me well."

"That's great. But you're not going yet?"

"I don't want to keep you from your studies," she said.

My emotions were boiling over. "Don't go yet. My studies can wait. I've missed you so much." I took her hand and drew her to me. She responded to my kisses more than I could ever have imagined.

"Darling Kate, I love you," I whispered in her ear.

"Farres, *habibi,* I think I'm in love with you too!"

She used the Arabic word for darling. I was on 'cloud nine' as they say. We hugged and kissed passionately as we sat on the bed together. I felt so happy I wanted to cry. It was the most wonderful feeling in the entire world.

There was a knock on the door. One of the girls in my group handed me some papers. She was surprised to see Kate sitting on my bed.

"Sorry, Farres. I didn't know you had a visitor."

"It's OK", I said. "Come and meet Kate."

She greeted Kate, then quickly disappeared, obviously embarrassed.

"Farres, I'm glad she interrupted. I really must go now."

"Kate, we have so much to say to each other."

"I will be in touch. Maybe you could visit my family?"

We sat in the car for a while longer. It was what I had been waiting for. An invitation to her home.

TWENTY

LONDON 1993

"For Goodness sake Knighty, calm down". Peter had never seen me so exuberant. I was running around like a chicken without a head. I wanted to shout from the rooftops, I wanted to dance and sing, I wanted to throw my arms around everyone. My stomach was in a flutter and my heart racing. Is this what it feels like to be in love, I said to myself. Did Kate feel the same, I wondered? I had to take hold of myself in order to continue cramming for exams, so it was a matter of extreme discipline. Kate said she would not attempt to see me before I finish. We did talk on the phone though, but not every day. Finally, the exams schedule was posted on the notice board and the next two weeks I worked harder than ever.

June arrived and my chestnut tree looked so beautiful. I had the urge to climb out of the window and jump into its branches and slide down the trunk. I had the urge to do many crazy things. Exams over and summer vacation would start soon. I wondered if I would come down with a bump, like people who take drugs are 'on high' for a while and then the blackness sends them into craving for more. God help such people, I thought.

189

I would miss the chestnut tree. For my second year I would have to look for a bedsit in a house shared with other students, but this, for me, would not be a new experience. Meanwhile, I had to look for a job, but first I had arranged with Kate to spend a weekend at her parents' home, north of London. She told me she would meet me in London at Kings Cross station, then we would take a different train going north. My excitement mounted with each station along the way. My stomach was turning somersaults. She was waiting for me at the bookstall where we had arranged and we decided to go for coffee while waiting for the next train. We kissed and walked along with our arms round each other. We were oblivious to all the other comings and goings of passengers, porters, traders, school children, people of all sorts and sizes, nationalities and backgrounds. I hesitated for a moment thinking of all the people who come to train stations. They were either being welcomed by family members or saying goodbye to their loved ones.

Here was I, a newcomer to England and missing my family, yet being welcomed into another family. At least, I hoped I would be welcome by her parents. She had given me every indication that I would be.

"Farres, I hope you will take to my parents," Kate said.

"What's more to the point, will they like me?" I responded.

"Of course," she said. "You are such a friendly person. Do you ever get rattled or angry?"

"Many times," I said. "I get angry at young people wasting their lives and their money. I get angry at the ignorance of English people who don't seem to know where Palestine is. Is it not the Holy Land where Christ lived? Are not the English people Christians?"

Kate smiled. "Most people are only interested in their own little lives, how to make money, how to enjoy themselves and where to go for holidays."

"Tell me about your family," I said.

"My father's name is Khalid, an Arab name, after his grandfather I suppose, though he was born in England and has never travelled to Palestine. His father, my grandfather, is Ibrahim. I am hoping that he and my grandmother will come and meet you. They live not far from my parents' home. My mother is Irish, as I told you, but she has lived in England since she was a little girl. There are lots of Irish people here."

"Where did your parents meet?" I asked her.

"I think it was in a bookstore where my Mother worked. My Dad's business has to do with publishing all kinds of books. You know, his grandfather worked for the British in Palestine before 1948. That's how they were able to come to England and were given British passports."

We chatted all the way on the train. I was excited and fascinated that she had a similar background to me, yet she looked and spoke totally British. In some ways, I felt as if I had known Kate all my life. I remember my first impressions of her as being sophisticated, business 'like and distant. She was not really like that at all. She was loving and caring. I wanted to hug her to bits.

A short walk from our destination took us to a labyrinth of streets, most of them similar in appearance; red-bricked semi-detached houses, with a small garden in front surrounded by a fence or hedges and another garden at the back. Kate led the way until we came to a house with rosebushes in the front garden and a door painted bright green. Kate laughed.

"Look," she said. "the green door tells you my mother is Irish and the name of the house tells you my father is Palestinian."

The name of the house was 'Haifa'.

Kate's mother had seen us coming and opened the door, welcoming us in.

"Farres, I've heard so much about you. It's so good to meet you at last," She kissed me on both cheeks. I was quite taken aback because English people usually only kiss on one cheek. She had blue eyes and reddish hair with streaks of grey, her figure robust but not fat. She was not at all like Kate, yet I sensed that she had the same loving disposition. Then Kate's father came in and shook my hand. Now I saw the resemblance to Kate, the same eyes and long straight nose. He addressed me in Arabic which surprised me, but then I learned that he didn't really know much of the language. I was then introduced to Kate's two sisters and a brother who were all much younger. I presented the family with a large box of chocolates.

"Thank you, thanks a lot. Did Kate tell you that it's her birthday tomorrow?" her father said.

I looked at Kate, slightly hurt. "Why didn't you tell me, *habibti*, that's really naughty of you."

"I didn't want you to buy…" she said.

Her mother sensed my disappointment. "Come on Farres, come with me. We must catch the shops before they shut." I had no time to even think about it before Kate's mother took my arm and bustled me out of the house, leaving Kate to argue with her father. It was a short walk to the shops during which her mother never stopped talking. I could hardly get a word in edgeways.

"Mrs. Zuayter, can you suggest something that Kate would really like?"

"Farres, please call me Janette. Kate likes chunky jewellery. Let's have a look…"

We looked at lots of necklaces in various colours of beads but somehow I couldn't see Kate wearing any of them. Perhaps her mother had different tastes. In the end I bought a silver chain with a heart-shaped locket, which gained Janette's approval. I had it gift wrapped and stuck it in my pocket. Then we did some grocery shopping and I carried the bag home for her. She was treating me like a son already but I had yet to propose!

Later, Kate and I took a walk around. It was a beautiful summer evening. We sat on a park bench, I held both her hands, and looked into her eyes.

"Kate, will you marry me?"

She withdrew her hands and got up, then stared at me with a look I had not seen before. For a split second I thought she was going to totally reject me.

"Are you really desperate to go to Palestine?" she asked.

I was confused. "Yes, why?"

"Do you really love me?" was her next question.

I pulled her down beside me and saw that her eyes were just about to brim over with tears. I couldn't understand her behaviour, but I took her head and buried it in my shoulder. "Darling Kate, you know I love you. I have told you many times."

"How can I be sure?"

"What more can I do to prove it to you," I said. "Shall I make love to you?"

"No".

"What is the matter? Don't you love me?"

"It's just that you keep talking about going to Palestine…" she hesitated. " I know that the only way you would be able to travel there is by obtaining a British passport."

I suddenly understood. She thought I had ulterior motives. By marrying Kate I would eventually have a British passport and be able to travel anywhere. With my present travel document as a Palestinian refugee I could never enter Palestine or Israel.

"My darling, what more can I say or do?"

193

I was hurt again. This was not a good start to the weekend.

We walked home in silence and Kate showed me the little back bedroom, which her mother had prepared for me. It was her brother's bedroom, with boyish posters of football heroes and racing cars stuck on the wall. I found it difficult to sleep, my body aching to take Kate into my arms, and racking my brain as to how I could convince her of my love yet I had to admit to myself that maybe there was a hidden motive of having a covetous desire to be able to travel to the homeland of my ancestors.

The next morning at breakfast, Janette sensed that there was some tension between us but did not probe. I greeted her cheerily and then all the family appeared, including Kate. Everyone sang 'Happy Birthday', piling on presents and cards on Kate's plate. I added my little jewellery box to the pile. She was almost afraid to open it. Perhaps she thought I had bought her an engagement ring. She seemed to be delighted with the necklace and gave me a big kiss on my cheek.

"Come on Farres. Give her a proper kiss," her brother shouted.

So, amidst clapping and whistling, I did just that. I noted that Kate had put extra eye make up on. Was it to conceal puffy eyes? I wondered.

Kate's grandparents arrived early for lunch. It was a special lunch for the birthday girl, her twenty-fifth birthday. My last birthday in January was my twenty-third, so Kate was a little older. I had been so looking forward to meeting Kate's grandparents and was not disappointed. They were delightful people, looking amazingly young and sprightly. Both spoke Arabic fluently, so we were totally oblivious of everyone else around us, as we sat and chatted.

"My family come from Jerusalem originally," said Kate's grandfather, but he went on: "However, my father was employed by the British Army and they moved him to Haifa. We had a beautiful villa in Haifa, with a large balcony and a garden. My mother was involved with all sorts of women's societies to help the poor, but we were reasonably well off."

"Why did you leave then?" I asked.

"There were many families leaving because we knew war was imminent and my parents were afraid that I would be involved in the fighting. My father somehow knew that the Arabs would be defeated and so he was afraid for my life."

"Did he know that the British were about to pack up and desert the Arabs?"

"Yes, of course, he knew, though he did not talk about it openly".

"So you remember everything?"

"I do indeed. I remember packing up all our belongings. I remember the furniture being taken away. I remember buying the tickets and boarding the ship at Haifa docks. We were only one family, there were many others."

"Why didn't you ever go back?" I asked.

"How could we face the Israelis? They robbed us of our land, property and everything. We still had a house in West Jerusalem. They stole that, too. Also, at first it was a struggle to settle down in London, to find a job and a place to live. Then after two years I met my dear wife," he took her hand as they sat side by side.

"She is also from Jerusalem but her family moved here several years before us."

"What was the worst thing about leaving?" I asked.

"My sister's face. She was newly married and was crying her eyes out when she saw us board the ship. Her husband's family came to see us off."

"What was your sister's name?" I suddenly went pale. I had heard a similar story before.

"It was Sawsan. I don't know what became of her. We wrote a few times but I don't think she received our letters."

"What was Sawsan's husband's name?" I asked. I was trembling.

"If I remember rightly it was Tha'er. They called him Abu Amin, even though he was newly married and did not have a son."

I put my hand on my mouth to prevent myself from screaming. I suddenly felt faint, yet so excited.

"Just a minute. My son has an old photograph somewhere." He got up to look for the album, while I sat utterly dumbstruck. Could it be that his sister Sawsan was the same Sawsan who gave birth to my father?

Just then, Kate came in, wiping her hands on her apron. "Lunch ready everyone," she announced. She saw my pale startled face. "What's up?"

I couldn't hold it in any longer. "Your grandfather has gone to look for a photo album. I think we are related."

"What? How?"

Her grandfather returned, holding an old faded album. They were all black and white pictures, mostly of London but there was one picture of a group taken in Haifa. The background was a ship with lots of people, but in the foreground was this group.

"A friend who was travelling with us took this picture," he said. "It was taken just before we were about to board the ship. This is me..." pointing to a smartly dressed young man. "I was eighteen. That is my sister, Sawsan. She was twenty." He pointed out a young woman, but her face was not clear, as she had it half buried in Tha'er's chest. She was much shorter than her husband who had his arms around her and was obviously trying to comfort her.

"That is my mother and father", he continued. I noticed the fancy hat his mother was wearing. "And those are my sister's in-laws." He pointed to a couple who seemed out of place. They were wearing peasant clothing like all village Palestinians wear. I scanned the picture closely. The woman with the long embroidered dress and head shawl looked tall and straight, holding her head up proudly. There was something familiar about her.

"I don't believe this. That's Granny Miriam." I shouted, startling everyone. I grabbed Kate, still in her apron and whirled around the floor with her, almost treading on her toes in my unconventional dance. Her mother came into the room.

"What on earth...?"

I explained that Kate's grandfather's sister was my grandmother, which made Kate and I second cousins, I supposed.

We all sat down to lunch but I did not take note of what we were eating. It was a mixture of English and Palestinian food. After this we sat drinking coffee and talked and talked. I told them all about Granny Miriam, my great-grandmother, who I remembered well. I told them my grand parents had died before I was born, but that I had heard stories about them from my father.

"Do you know," I said. "When that photograph was taken Sawsan must have been pregnant with my father." They all gasped when they realised the significance of it all.

"My father was born on their way to Lebanon, before they reached the border," I informed them. My heart was racing with surprise and excitement. The co-incidence was unreal. No one would believe me. I felt as if the world had suddenly become very small and that Kate was already part of my life. It was all too much to comprehend. I went on to tell them about Shatila camp, about my mother, about my sister and the massacre, about my other two sisters, about my father being deported to Tunis and then finding his way back to Lebanon. There was so much to tell them.

"Tell me more about my sister," said Kate's grandfather. I could see his eyes were misty and his hands trembling as he was squeezing one of my hands, the other one holding on to his wife. She was also looking very emotional with wide astonished eyes.

"Well, as I said, she died before I was born. Conditions in the refugee camp were primitive in the extreme. For the first year and a half they lived in tents without running water or sanitation. By what you tell me Sawsan had lived a comfortable life in Haifa, so it is not surprising that she died young. Apparently she died giving birth to her third child, but her second child died, so my father didn't have any siblings."

He sighed. "Poor, poor, Sawsan. We tried to persuade her to come with us, but she was in love with your grandfather. There's no doubt about that. Fancy, Granny Miriam survived them all. She must have been a very strong woman."

"Yes, she became a mother to my father," said I. "She died in 1982 just before the massacre."

When Kate's grandparents eventually went home we were all utterly exhausted, not from running around but from the astounding and unexplained mystery of meeting Kate and all the emotions it had aroused.

* * * *

"You are so lucky having your parents and grandparents," I said to Kate, later.

"Yes, I can see that your family have suffered so much," she said. "I also saw a lot of suffering when I went to Palestine recently."

"I must write to my father straight away. He will be amazed," I said. "But first I want to ask you the same question Kate. Will you marry me?"

"Oh Farres, darling, I will," she said, her lips reaching for mine. What more could I want? It was the happiest day of my life.

Monday morning and it was time to say goodbye. Kate drove me as far as the newspaper office where she worked, then I took the underground to St. Paul's. My first goal was to talk to Dr. Tom, so I made a beeline for the hospital. I had called him to say I wanted to tell him some important news, but did not divulge what it was. We sat and drank coffee in the little cafeteria of the hospital. He was not surprised about my engagement but very surprised to hear the coincidence of our relationship, and the history behind it. I could see that he was pleased but warned me not to slacken off in my studies. I asked him to tell Sally.

"No, no," he said. "You have to tell Sally yourself. She might be a bit jealous." He laughed.

Next I had to tell Ali, who was also getting involved in a relationship with an English girl. Finally, I returned to Medical School and went with Peter to look for lodgings for our second academic year.

TWENTY ONE

"Sir, will you please come with me." A passport official was leading me away to a little room apart at Ben Gurion Airport, Tel Aviv. Kate and our little daughter, Miriam, were told to wait, not to follow me. I could hear my daughter pleading:

"Daddy, Daddy, where are you going? Don't leave us."

"Don't worry darling. I'm coming back," I shouted.

"Sir, I see you were born in Lebanon." He scanned my British passport carefully, page by page.

"Yes."

"Do you have a Lebanese passport?"

"No." I was not going to supply any information.

"Why not?"

"I am not Lebanese."

"What are you then?"

"I am British."

"Sir, I see you have a British passport but not a British name."

"That's true."

He eyed me with a cold look. "You must cooperate with us. It is for your own security."

"I understand."

"Have you been to Israel before?"

"No."

I began to feel sorry for the poor Israeli security officer. He was only doing his job, after all. He was getting more and more frustrated at my inadequate answers. He then decided to examine all the luggage, turning out every little item even to our toothbrushes and sending them to be X-rayed. He told me to take off my shoes and sent them to be X-rayed. I was beginning to feel angry. Finally he turned to me.

"What do you intend to do in Israel?"

"I told you. I am a doctor and I have been invited to attend a Symposium with the title: 'Analysis of genetic defects in the newborn'." I showed him the letter of invitation with a Jerusalem address on the paper.

"You can go now sir. Enjoy your time in Israel."

Phew, I took in a deep breath and expired slowly from my mouth. Rejoining the family, Kate took over wheeling the trolley, while I picked up Miriam to carry her.

" Was it so bad?" asked Kate.

"Yes, it was humiliating. I remember when I arrived in London ten years ago. There I was welcomed without question."

We walked through the exit and immediately spotted a man holding up a placard:

'Dr. Kassem'. He greeted us warmly and drove us to our hotel in Jerusalem.

I was in Palestine, in Jerusalem. I had to pinch myself to make sure I wasn't dreaming.

* * * *

Kate and I were married in the spring of 1994. She had graduated and had found a new job in the area of the Medical School, so we were able to rent a small apartment, basic but comfortable. Meanwhile I continued with my medical studies, the third year being quite different and mixing in with a completely different group of students. We spent a lot of time in the hospital, examining patients and given bedside teaching, attending clinics, observing surgical operations, learning the mechanics of taking blood samples, measuring blood pressures, inserting urethral catheters and even helping to deliver babies.

I thanked God daily for having Kate at my side to support and encourage. I made many mistakes and failed some of the tests, but she would always be there for me. Tom, too was a great help and comfort when I felt discouraged. I finally graduated with an MBBS in 1997 and now was working towards a degree in Paediatrics. It had been a long slog but I had made it.

Our adorable daughter, named of course, after Granny, was born towards the end of 1996.

* * * *

It was June in Jerusalem and although only the beginning of summer, the land already looked parched. One thing, I thought, we didn't have to worry about taking an umbrella with us. No wonder England always looked so lusciously green. It never stopped raining there. At least that was the impression I had.

Everyone greeted us with 'Shalom, welcome to Israel'. I was surprised that even some of the Arab traders in the Old City greeted us with 'Shalom' until I returned their greeting in Arabic *'Salaam alaikum'*. This is Palestine, not Israel, I reminded them. They smiled at my naiveté. Perhaps they thought we were Jews or American tourists who didn't know the difference.

However at the Medical Conference, held in a Jewish hospital I had to be more careful with my vocabulary and tended to keep to English.

There were both Arab and Jewish doctors attending the lectures and it was very informative and enlightening. For me, too, it was a whole new cultural experience. I was glad to meet Jewish doctors who were not totally in love with the Zionist dream, and I was very impressed by all the latest technology and medical equipment. The hospital, too, was spotless, far cleaner than the English hospitals I had worked in. But then, I reminded myself, the buildings were also more new and modern.

Our next plan was to go to Galilee. I had dreamed of this ever since I was a little boy, in fact, ever since Granny had presented the worry beads to me. I calculated quickly. Eighteen years! If I counted the years that Granny had possessed them it made them 78 years old. I had carried them with me wherever I went. I think Kate found it rather amusing that I attached so much importance to them.

"Those beads have become a good luck fetish for you," she said one day.

"Not at all," I argued. "They are just a reminder of our ancestry in Palestine and our close connection with the Christian heritage also."

Now, in Palestine, I was going to put them to rest, as it were.

We decided to hire a car, so as not to be dependent on public transport, but we were not used to driving on the right hand side of the road and the traffic was at times terrifying. It was a straight route from Jerusalem to Haifa along the coastal highway and we were there in less than three hours including the necessary toilet stops along the way. Haifa is a big bustling city set on a hill sloping down to the sea. The population is a mixture of Jews, Christians and Muslims. I was surprised to see so many Arabs there. We found an Arab restaurant selling kebabs, *homous* and other dishes which made me quite homesick for Shatila, and we rested while studying a map of the region. We had also brought with us a very old map with the names of all the villages, which had existed before 1948. Comparing the two maps, it was uncanny to see that most of the Arab villages had disappeared off the map or were replaced by Hebrew names.

"Look, Kate," I said, as Miriam climbed on to my lap, "where has the village of Al-Tira gone?" There was no such village. "That's where Granny Miriam and her family lived," I said. We asked the waiters at the restaurant, but they were young men and had no idea about the location of the old villages. Then we saw a group of old men, wearing keffiyehs and sitting at a table, smoking their arguilehs or water-pipes. The sun was shining on the coloured glass bottles, playing patterns on the whitewashed walls. Miriam was fascinated watching the colours dance around the walls. She was giggling with delight.

"Why don't we ask those old men over there?" Kate suggested.

I approached them, speaking Arabic. They drew up another stool for me to join them, welcoming me into their little circle. I showed them my old map.

"Can you tell me where I can find the village of Al-Tira?" I asked.

They carefully scanned the map and shook their heads. However, one of them, older than the other two, said, "Yes, maybe I remember."

"Do you really?" I said. "How come you did not leave in 1948 when all Palestinians were thrown out?"

"Ah," he said, "my parents and I left Haifa for a short while but we were allowed back. We did not leave the country. I have lived in Haifa most of my life."

"So you are an Israeli citizen now", I asked. This was news to me.

"Yes," he said, "but we do not have the full benefits and privileges as the Jewish Israelis."

"Is it far to the location of this old Arab village?"

"About six miles," he said, pointing out the way. "It's uphill most of the way. Look out for bushes of prickly pears. Wherever there are bushes of prickly pears or cactus fruit, as some call them, there used to be an Arab village."

"Are there still olive trees, too?"

He laughed. "No, you'd be lucky to find any olive trees. The Israelis dug them up. They probably replanted them in their settlements."

I thanked him and returned to Kate. "We have to look out for *saber.*"

"What's that Daddy?" said Miriam, looking rather sleepy.

"It is a fruit that is very sweet, but impossible to pick because the skin is covered in very prickly burrs. If you get one of these tiny thorns in your skin, it will drive you mad!"

"You are exaggerating, as usual," laughed Kate.

"No, I'm not. I'm perfectly serious. Do you know what *saber* means. It means 'patience' and that is what we need right now," I said laughing, and getting up to walk to the car. We got into the car and Miriam was asleep within minutes of strapping her into her kiddiseat at the back. Kate was still curious about the fruit.

"How do the women pick this fruit and what do they taste like?" she asked.

"The older village women have a knack of picking them to avoid the prickles. Outside the fruit is green but inside it is bright orangey-red, full of seeds, which you eat, very squashy and very delicious," I informed her.

"Mmn, sounds good."

We continued on our way uphill, passing clusters of houses and apartment blocks, interspersed with rows of eucalyptus trees and pine trees. We saw a few people but when we asked the way, speaking in English, they shook their heads. "No Hebrew?" they asked. There were fields of planted corn and wheat and other crops but no sign of clumps of prickly pear bushes. I calculated that we had gone about six miles, so

I parked the car on some waste ground and we decided to walk around. There was noone about as far as we could see. I carried Miriam and gently woke her up. We walked along some dirt paths for about half a mile until we came to a large clump of pine trees. There were piles of rocks in places but they did not appear to be from ruined buildings. Suddenly I spotted several shrubs of Cacti. The fruit was still small and unripe but I recognised the bushes immediately. We looked around. There were no signposts, no ruins of mosques or churches, not even piles of stones to indicate that there had once been a thriving Arab community in this area.

"I wonder if this is it?" I said to Kate.

"Well, I guess all the Arab villages that were destroyed resemble this piece of ground, so there is no way we can be sure of the exact location," she replied.

It was just a piece of waste ground. Some people had even used it to dump their rubbish. Maybe this was it, maybe not.

"What shall we do?" I said.

"Let us think that we have found it. We could spend another whole day looking, and we shall never be sure. None of the people living round here will know. They are probably all Jewish immigrants, anyway."

Kate was right. We decided to bury our little treasure before the daylight faded.

"What are you going to do, Daddy?" said Miriam.

I showed her the old beads; their colours really faded, and explained to her that her great-great grandmother Miriam used to live here and she gave me these beads when I was a little boy and because Granny Miriam was buried in Lebanon, these beads were symbolic of her return to Palestine. It was too complicated for her to understand.

"I will explain more when you are older, darling," I told her.

I had bought a small gardening trowel in Jerusalem and so I dug a shallow hole and 'planted' the beads. My face was wet with tears and sweat.

"Why are you crying, Daddy?"

"Just remembering…" Just then two men suddenly appeared, scowling at us.

I decided to play it cool. "Shalom," I said, smiling.

They replied with a barrage of Hebrew words, waving their arms about and pointing us to the road. We were obviously not welcome, even on a piece of waste ground.

We quickly made our way back to the car and drove off down the hill.

"When are we going home, Daddy?"

"Don't you like it here, darling?" I asked Miriam.

"No, I don't understand what people say and they make me frightened."

I could understand her childish fears but I had so looked forward to showing her Palestine.

"You will be going home very soon with Mummy, but Daddy has some work to do.

Our plan was that after this trip, Kate and Miriam would return to London while I stayed on a few months longer to help in the Clinics of the Palestinian refugee camps on the West Bank.

For now though we had to visit Nazareth, an Arab town, where for sure we would be welcome. The day after tomorrow was going to be another very special day.

* * * *

Church bells and the muezzin call to prayer were sounding out simultaneously, at times synchronising but mostly discordant. I looked out of the Hotel window to see that we were within a few yards of both a church and a mosque. Perhaps it means that it was time to pray to God whatever our faith, I reflected. Anyway it was time to get up. We had an important day ahead of us, and I was as excited as a little boy.

We had seen the news on television a month ago. After nearly two decades of occupation, the Israeli army had finally left Southern Lebanon, taking with them their allies considered to be traitors by the Lebanese, into Israel. The barbed wire border fence was still in place and the Israeli army still patrolling the border from their side, but the Lebanese and Palestinians in the southern camps freed. It had been a time of great celebration for them and some refugees from Shatila had come south to stretch their arms through the barbed wire to greet Palestinians on the Israeli side. We heard, too, that when they bolted and padlocked the last gate, they called it 'Fatima's Gate'. How ironic, I thought. The name of my murdered sister.

I knew it would be impossible to telephone my father from Israel but in this age of modern technology, it was possible to get a message through to him by e-mail. So when I was in Jerusalem I had e-mailed a friend in Shatila to pass a message on to my father that we would hopefully be at the border on the last Friday of June.

Today was that day. Would my family be there the other side of the border? Would we be able to touch hands? Or at least wave to them? The suspense was almost unbearable. I wasn't sure whether to tell Miriam or not. Suppose we were going to be disappointed? I couldn't keep it any longer.

"Miriam, darling, wake up. We may be going to see your Grandpa today."

"Back to London?"

"No, your other grandfather, my father, Grandpa Amin."

She rubbed her eyes. "Really, Daddy?"

"Maybe." I said. "*Inshallah*, if God wills."

This was exciting news. I prayed that she would not be disappointed. Kate, of course was also excited. In a way it was her family too and not just because she was married to me.

After breakfast, we had the car checked and taking some sandwiches with us we set off, first towards Haifa, then a road going north to the border. We had to park the car in a tourist rest stop, then walked the rest of the way towards the barbed wire fence. Kate was wearing her jeans, but Miriam had a short skirt and T-shirt. The prickly bushes scratched her legs, so I carried her. The Israeli army looked at us suspiciously but we were not the only people making for the border fence. We waited and watched, looking up and down the fence. We sat down on the stony ground to wait.

After about half an hour we spied an old rickety bus in the distance disgorging its passengers. There were old men with crutches, old women, young boys and girls, small children holding hands with their parents, far more people it seemed to me than the old bus could contain. They ran, waving flags, dancing and singing towards the fence. At first I did not recognize anyone, but my father saw me first. He tried to shout but his tears were choking him.

"Farres, Farres, at last, my son, my son, *habibi*, my son…"

I too, was choking with tears. "Baba," I screamed. With all this commotion and emotion, Miriam was frightened and started to scream, burying her face in my shoulder. When I could see through my tears, there was a crowd to greet us, not just my father but my sisters, their husbands and children, my stepmother and brother, now a schoolboy, looking as cheeky as I was at his age but not remembering me. We stretched our hands through the wire, not minding the trickles of blood from the barbs. It didn't matter how much we were going to get scratched.

"*Mabruk, mabruk,* congratulations Farres. You are a doctor now," they cried in unison.

"This is my darling Kate," I said, in Arabic, to my father. He tried to put his face through the fence to kiss her. Instead he kissed his hand and pushed it through the wire, touching her face with his kiss and taking hold of her arm, not just her hand.

"I am so happy to see you," he said, "and your daughter, too." He longed to be able to touch Miriam but she was still very frightened. It was like a competition as to who could shout the loudest. I wanted to ask them how everyone was, Auntie, Uncle, my cousins, neighbours, friends. They, too, had a barrage of questions to ask me.

"How is Lucy? Do you ever see her? Is she still alive?"

"Yes, I visit Lucy quite often. She wanted to come with us but she cannot walk any more. She sends you her love and her prayers."

"Give her my love and prayers, too." I shouted back to my father.

I noticed my father's face was not much different but his hands were definitely not so young looking. Then I figured of course that he is the same age as the Palestinian exile, which was fifty-two years ago.

Some of the people were filling paper cups of earth from the Palestinian side to give to those in Lebanon. Others were joining hands and singing national songs, dancing around in circles and waving the Palestinian flag.

"Come back to us soon. Shatila is waiting for you," my father shouted.

"I will come back as soon as I get my full degree as a children's doctor," I shouted back.

"We all love you, Farres," they chorused.

I blew them all a kiss and waved frantically.

Meanwhile, the Israelis were getting more and more agitated with all the noise. They started revving up the engines of their jeeps and shooting into the air to frighten us. Finally they came and physically pushed us away from the fence. We were still waving wildly as we slowly walked away backwards.

We returned to the car and just sat in it, not wanting even to talk. It had been an overwhelming emotional experience. I wept like a child while Kate tried to comfort me. They were tears of thankfulness and hope for the future. I was looking forward now to seeing the conditions of the refugee camps on the West Bank and finding out first hand what was needed to relieve their sufferings and give them some hope for the future.

Printed in the United Kingdom
by Lightning Source UK Ltd.
121915UK00001B/418/A